Th
A journey into the Dark Side
By
Claire Manning

Published by Claire Manning at Amazon

Chapter 1

Montreal City, winter 2012

Situated between Champ-de-Mars and Place-d'Armes metro stations, the Montreal Superior Court on Notre-Dame street East had several courtrooms, one of which had a particular case ongoing on which the media had been focusing their attention for months. This trial had made the headlines as Montreal's trial of the century. They had been many other class action suits in the past in the city but this one was like no other.

All Rise! Announced a court clerk inviting everyone to stand as a white haired and bearded man dressed in a black robe entered and walked up the few stairs which ended at a raised platform. Justice Mercier, who was overseeing this class action case, looked over the crowded court room where more than a dozen court reporters were seated in their reserved media area on the ready to note everything that would happen this very important day.

They were more than eager to record everything that would be said during the trial. The pressure was on them as thousands of people were expecting them to provide the information due to the fact that the court proceedings would not be televised. It had been a highly mediatised criminal case aiming at the prosecution of a financial icon and business man as well as his wife.

Alfonzo Pinocchia and Martina Di Salvo were accused of having used their investment company to commit embezzlement and misappropriation of real estate properties belonging to very affluent personalities worth of billions of dollars.

The dozen members of the jury composed of six women and six men were standing, feeling uneasy due to the very intimidating looks from some of the victim's sympathisers that were purposely directed toward them in order to assist them in coming up with what they regarded as the only logical and right verdict of guilty on all counts. The more aggressive had taken the seats that were the closest ones to the jury members.

There was some applause when the three lawyers representing the hundreds of plaintiffs in fighting for their cause took their seats on the front left side of the judge's bench and pulled a great deal of documents from their wheeled briefcases. By their looks, these prosecutors were displaying their determination to aggressively fight to win the case and obtain justice for their clients. One of them seemed to be the leader as being much older and very icy looking. The two other lawyers were in their early forties and projected a softer side than their leader.

Then, everything changed in a split second as Alfonzo Pinocchia pushing his handicapped wife in a wheelchair, along with three top Montreal lawyers of the La Prosperità Firm entered the judicial arena down the center aisle. A court clerk indicated the table assigned to them which was situated to the front, right of the judge's bench. Alfonzo Pinocchia, now a much older men who had lost, along with his reputation of running a very successful business, his youth and good looks. Time had taken its toll. He was no longer the man to whom many women had dedicated their lives in order to win the ultimate prize of becoming his spouse. With time, Pinocchia looked to have become another man.

Boos and shouts could be heard from the very angry crowd as they watched his lawyers walking down the center aisle with their high end leather briefcases. They seemed to be living in a different era than the rest of the crowd. They all wore tailor made suits with gold cuff links and tie pins shinning away. These men looked like typical movie and TV portrayals of Mafioso. They wore heavy scented cologne which made people react immediately as they walked down the aisle to the front of the court room. They were the top lawyers of the firm: La Prosperità in Montreal. They had extended their business into every major city in Canada, the USA and Europe. Pinocchia kept his awkward smile all the way to the table showing his defiance to the "already made opinions" from the crowd. His unique and renowned branding of himself, a red rose attached to the left lapel of his suit jacket was the only thing that outshone his cold regard towards the crowd. Martina kept her emotions to herself.

The beautiful woman was impeccably made-up with her hair stylishly braided around her head. She worn a chic dark blue jacket, and she was, without a doubt, the most elegant woman in the courtroom. Her legs were covered with a simple plaid blanket. She looked straight at the judge's desk on the raised platform, seemingly giving the impression that she would never surrender herself to suffer the consequences of an unfair trial.

As they arrived at their defense table, a young man entered the courtroom, dragging two heavy wheeled briefcases, unloaded piles of documents and placed them on the table in a very orderly fashion. He didn't wait for a graceful appreciation for what he had just done; he just expressively indicated that his job was done and walked out of the court room.

As the lawyers examined their folders and documents, their very shiny gold Rolex watches certainly branded them. They had gained throughout decades due to their work the reputation of being the best defence lawyers of the whole country. These men had a very high rate of success in winning court cases and included among those were some of the most infamous crooks the country had ever known. The courtroom clerk then walked to his seat near the judge.
Please be seated, said Justice Mercier. He stomped his gavel several times for order as the crowd didn't stop muttering hysterically.

When everything finally quieted down as the banging of the wood gavel echoed through the now silent court room, the judge saw that the time had arrived to invite Mr. Millburn, the prosecutor of the court to recite the charges against Mr. Pinocchia.

- Please come forward and make your statements, Mr. Millburn

- Thank you very much Your Honor, we will now proceed with the case of Mr. and Mrs Pinocchia, accused of embezzlement from investors in the amount of billions of American dollars. Here is the list of all the accusations being presented before the court on this day, Tuesday, December 1st, 2012.

- The Pinocchia's have unlawfully benefited from their client's monetary investments and have taken away their hard earned money along with very expensive properties throughout the Bahamas, Caribbean Islands and several cities in Canada and also Europe and Asia which they have sold or appropriated for themselves without their client's awareness. They have committed crimes and today, the reason why they are sitting in this courtroom on trial is due to the crimes they have committed:

Theft, fraud, forgery and uttering forged documents, false pretense, identity theft, money laundering and receiving the proceeds of crime. Your Honor, without further delay, I'd like to call several witnesses to the bench.

The judge agreed that the prosecutors proceed and call all their witnesses, one after the other, who were to come before the court to testify that they had factually been ripped off of their retirement savings, grandchildren's scholarship investments and their real estate properties which in most cases were their dream homes in which they planned to later retire.

- We will elaborate further on these points during the procedures but I wanted everyone in this room to understand that we are not dealing with an insignificant case here. The Pinocchia are professional white collar criminals and with their unsurpassed seducing lies, they are the best in the business, they have duped a tremendous amount of honest people who are now suffering and have had their lives ruined due to them.

- These people have lost their homes and wealth, they now have to survive from check to check, and the more elderly ones now have to live on their old age pensions which as you all know amount to very little. They have lost their dreams and all benefits from a lifetime hard work. The Pinocchia have cowardly stolen their dreams.
- I am submitting all the written reports and statements from each one the Pinocchia's victims which undeniably and clearly denounce their crimes. Your Honor, I'd like to first expose the incidents with a time line so that you and the jury will all understand what we are dealing with.

- Mr. Pinocchia's so called "financial operation" has lasted well over a decade allowing him to accumulate tremendous wealth at the expense of his victims. Along with what I have already presented to you, I am submitting to you all the writs of seizure which include seizure of Mr. Pinocchia's properties.

- These include all of their bank accounts related to these criminal financial activities, material assets, his vintage car collection, real estate properties we have included the seizure documents for luxury condo buildings situated in the Griffin district of Montreal and others in downtown Miami.

Taking all the substantial amount of documents, a court clerk announced, handing them to the judge's assistant documenting the prosecutor's reports of all the witness's testimonies.

- They are crooks! Where is our money? They have ruined our lives! Jail these animals for life! They should be hanged! Some of Pinocchias victims screamed in the court.

- Order! Order! Order! Said the judge, you will not be allowed to remain in the courtroom if you carry on this way. This is my last warning; I will have order in my court. If you do not obey the court rules, you will be escorted out immediately! I will clear the court room! Understand that we will proceed with the current laws of the country and the intention here is to give a fair trial!

The judge couldn't stop banging his gavel as the shouts became louder and louder. The court had become a madhouse per the judge's observation.
A few Pinocchia's victims, including a woman with a very strong German accent who seemed to be accompanied of members of her family were escorted out the court room as the judge's warnings didn't convince them to remain silent while being in the presence of the criminals who had ruined their lives.

Everyone could feel the electrical tension inside the courtroom. It was a very controversial case that the media had continually fueled in all the news outlets including conspiracies, disturbing Pinocchia connections to Italian mafia from Sicily with dots connected to certain Montreal gangs.

The amount of speculation related to this case was out of the ordinary. People had greatly suffered mentally and physically and were counting on the lawyers assigned to this case to save them from more distress.

Chapter 2

The Pinocchia family

Alfonzo Pinocchia had a very prosperous financial company. He had become a hero also within Montreal high society amongst the Italian elite including the mafia. He had been recognized as a mogul of generosity within a circle of family and friends. His reputation was that of a man who wore his heart on his sleeve, ready to respond to the cries of the poor and needy, particularly during Christmas and the holidays.

Boxes of goods, toys and food literally poured into several Goodwill locations and food banks. He always contributed to the causes anonymously but due to his unprecedented generosity, many suspected that he was behind this.

Alfonzo was born in the mid-seventies in the very poor neighborhood of Little Italy in Montreal where his immigrant family had settled into the country of their dreams and had very humble beginnings. Many Sicilian families had resettled in the city for a better economic life.

His father Alessandro and his mother Elena had opened a pizzeria on St-Laurent blvd, known as the Main. They were very honest hard working people.

They didn't take a break from work. The pizzeria was opened 7 days a week. Later, during the following years, several of their relatives and friends had joined the family business as soon as they earned their immigration status. It had truly become a family affair.

It didn't take very long for the IL Sicilian restaurant to become famous for its various types of pizza crusts and particular blending of flavours, with the sizzling sounds and flavourful smoke coming from a huge wood burning stove chimney, it became the show piece of the neighborhood.

The restaurant had been built with an open concept where everyone could see Alfonzo's father and assistants swirling the dough, adding the key ingredients to create the perfect pizza and watch them deposit this mouth-watering piece of art into the magical inferno.

The irresistible aroma floating outside the restaurant from the chimney ignited and excited the taste buds of anyone walking in the neighborhood. The restaurant had huge windows and people couldn't resist slowing and looking through the windows at the cooks skillfully showing off their talents.

They could see that the customers and employees were enjoying their time. Glasses of wine were lifted in the air, everyone wishing that the good times could carry on for the rest of their lives. The atmosphere inside the restaurant produced a feeling of having for a few hours been magically teleported to Sicily, the island that they loved so much.

For the Italian community living at the time in Montreal, it definitely reminded them of their unique Catania city neighbourhood where several pizzeria owners were busy from early morning, preparing the key ingredients along with employees signing their best interpretations of popular soprano operas of the time.

Despite the unparalleled opportunities offered by their new adopted country, the healing process of having to leave their country took time for these new immigrants who still had to overcome this homesick feeling. Some had wished to return to their mother country but time had been economically difficult in this part of the world. Now having this particular place to gather in order to enjoy food and ambiance, it had become a beneficial process in healing the nostalgia many had felt since their arrival in their new country.

Along with the food that was by far the best in town, the atmosphere of the whole place made it so special that the restaurant had to expand in order to respond to the great demand from the patrons; not only for dining in but also for delivery. He had to do something as he was in a situation where he was losing lots of business due to not being able to fulfil the increasing demand.

Finally, Alfonzo's father, using his incredibly convincing and very strong Sicilian character bought out the two businesses which were his neighbors in the building. It didn't however go without a fight. The popularity of IL Sicilian restaurant benefited them tremendously and they didn't want to give up easily what they now foresaw as being a gold mine for them. Alfonzo's father was a very pragmatic and charismatic man. While he was not a large man his charm and talent along with a tremendous amount of cash made it hard to resist him.

This was the first lesson Alfonzo had learned from his father, watching him speaking and gesturing with his hands, expressing that he was a man possessed of great self-confidence that made him seem quite intimidating to others. He used this along with his persistence to convince his neighboring merchants that this was the way to go. He took over the whole building. Shortly after this time, Alfonzo felt that something had happened that changed his father. He never seemed to be completely happy and relaxed at work since that time.

- "Where there is money my son, there is a will! Never forget about that".

After this point, the business became even more prosperous and this is where at a young age that Alfonzo learned the art of making the best pizza in town. Alfonzo was eager to help his parents and they taught him the particular and unique crafting to make a perfect pizza.

He learned the secret of how to make a perfect dough, how to make and spread their unique homemade spicy tomato sauce that was gently boiled in a huge cast iron pot over the stove for hours, how to marry the perfect cheeses with the various other ingredients including pepperoni, onions, anchovies, garlic, herbs, peppers, spices and olive oil. His father succeeded in being able to import all the ingredients from Sicily; the real deal as he called them.

People wondered at his ability to import the real original Sicilian products that nobody else seemed to be able to import into the country.

Nowhere else in the city or even in the country could anyone have a more authentic taste of Sicily than at The IL Sicilian. Round or square, every pizza was handcrafted with love.

The family's religious roots showed in the candles on each table and Christian pictures on the walls thorough the restaurant that were part of the decor. Sicilian songs from renowned sopranos of the country were being heard from mismatched speakers hanging from various locations on the restaurant's ceiling. An entire wall displayed the tremendous variety of wine bottles that his father had imported.

With time, the maple hardwood floor started to show several scratches and distinctive lines which increased as the number of clients increased. It was a clear proof that the place was absolutely buzzing.

The table cloths ranged from humble cotton squares to beautiful and unique linen or white linen tablecloths, their borders showing very fancy crocheted lace or netting. They were all covered with a very thin plastic shield. Alfonzo's father and mother made it a place where people gathered to enjoy this unique Sicilian ambiance and food.

As he grew up, Alfonzo graduated from high school and made the decision that he was not going to stay in the pizzeria business. Despite the fact that the money was very good, his father, while disappointed with his decision of not taking over the family business, understood his son's dream to become a financial entrepreneur and was happy that he would make his way in life and have a good living. After all, this is what his father had wished for when immigrating to this country.

Along with liking money a lot, he often contemplated visiting Sicilia, the country of his origin and to connect with this beautiful island that his parents had talked about so many times.
Between business trips, he had always managed to make a stop on the island. He became more in tune with the people, its unique beauty and its customs along the way, he had this sentiment that he felt more at home there than in Montreal.

Chapter 3

Alfonzo Pinocchia's destiny

A few years later, having established his company named "Dream Investments" not only had he made major headway in his financial enterprise; Alfonzo had become a very handsome man sought often by the ladies. His hard work at the pizzeria had sculptured his body; he had become a very attractive man.

While he had his father's facial features, he was a much taller man than his dad. His height and charm came from his mother who had all the characteristics of a real Hollywood femme fatale. He soon became the new "Valentino" of the neighborhood and many women of all ages fell for him.

Always wearing impeccable black or dark blue tailor made suits, he never was without a red rose on the left side of his jacket. It had become his personal branding. Nowhere did he go, not to any social gathering that he did not have this contrasting color feature on his suit jacket. With his brown piercing eyes, not a woman could resist his very unique and provoking advances.

He had built a harem of mistresses of all ages under false promises of a better future for all of them, handing out a few gifts of diamond rings and other favours in exchange for their fidelity. His favorite club where he used to meet women was Blvd44 on St-Laurent situated not too far from his father's pizzeria.

He had his reputation made and within the circle of high profile and rich people, he was venerated, not only for being a very wealthy man and having enriched many, but as the alpha male of the city by the ladies. Many business men of the area envied his sex appeal and popularity. Alfonzo was simply irresistible.

Money was abundant; women were falling for him. Life was good, he couldn't have asked for better.

Chapter 4

The Cornucopia effect

His business expanded and required less of his direct supervision as he had put together a very skilled and strong executive team, Alfonzo gradually extended his vacation time. He had delegated his business to very loyal employees who enjoyed working for him as they were more than generously remunerated. Compared to any other existing multi-national companies in the same business around the world, they were the most highly paid.

Alfonzo would fly to Sicily and enjoy his time on the Mediterranean. He soon acquired a $40M 217.85ft OKTO yacht; the most expensive and luxurious ship of its kind to sail the blue Mediterranean Sea. As he was sailed on the ocean, the yacht turned many heads and created wonders as to who could ever afford to own it. The beautiful Monaco scenery of the famous and elite's boats were by far outweighed by this one of a kind new luxurious yacht.

The ship had 2 master staterooms, a Jacuzzi/pool on the sundeck, a guest elevator, a large tender garage that converted to a beach club or a gym; it had 8,000 square feet of living space, the panoramic sky lounge with vaulted ceilings reaching nearly 10 feet in height. 11 people could comfortably enjoy living on the ship as well as the crew. Only the best of everything was served on his yacht.

Excellence in everything had become his brand. Exotic food, top of the line Champagne and wines; everything was served on Flora Danica Dinner servings that had delicate carvings and 24-carat gold accents with rich, hand-painted botanical motifs. Only the finest wines were served in crystal glasses. He had an Executive Chef, a Sous Chef and a pastry Chef. They were available 24/7 to satisfy the most perfectionist palates who would be in the ready for their service, even on a short notice.

Local musicians were hired for the duration of his vacation and performed every evening with a broad spectrum of opera and instrumental classical music while Alfonzo and his guests enjoyed their liquors and $4,500 of King of Denmark cigars around the pool on the sundeck.

Alfonzo had now reached a new level of existence that he had never suspected existed. Within this world of business classes, he had become part of the elite, of the wealthiest and famous people in the business world. With these new contacts, he would soon exceed even his own prediction and positively influence the market to new heights, looking forward to creating excellence and abundance for his investors.

It was not rare to see men accompanied by beautiful women, some highly priced escorts visiting Alfonzo's yacht. Everything was allowed as long as it was kept in secret to protect their reputations. Having more money that he would know what to do with it, Alfonzo had however become a very selective man as the years went by; as to whom he would invite to join him on his yacht. One of the reasons, along with his undeniable penchant for big spending, is that he had become an undisciplined gambler. As he took to his new addiction, he turned his vacation time into gambling time.

The more money he lost gambling, the more seemed to arrive in his bank account. The law of giving and receiving in return applied to him to the letter.

Alfonzo had become a popular icon recognized worldwide by many organizations as a great philanthropist, a generous donor who had an appreciation for money but at the same time recognized that wealth had to be shared if he wanted his life style to last.

He was grateful for his good fortune and strongly believed that he was blessed by the endless horn of plenty, the Cornucopia, provided to people who have showed leadership and worked hard to earn their financial power.
Alessandro and Elena Pinocchia couldn't be more proud of their unique son. He made his way by first dreaming big and then turning these dreams in reality, materialized a great business and it paid off.

While Alfonzo insisted several times that his parents sell the restaurant and retire to enjoy everything that life could now offer them with his fortune, they refused to retire and kept the business going at their restaurant. It was too hard to leave their way of life.

They were attached to their long time clientele and the unique atmosphere this restaurant provided for them. They felt at home away from home.

After several trip vacations to Sicily, Alfonzo had soon been introduced to several successful business men of the area, he would dock his yacht near his Cala Mosche beach where access to pedestrians was very limited and quiet. There were no bars or sun loungers or sellers to be seen around. It was the perfect quiet, little-known sandy beach for someone like him who was seeking a peaceful location for his relaxation and private meetings.

As he very much enjoyed this area of the island, he finally made a deal with the city to buy part of the beach and make it a very private spot for him.

He was questioned as to how at such a young age he had earned his fortune; others wanted to know his rules for success, etc.
Alfonzo felt completely in heaven to be so admired by so many. His ego grew exponentially.

Dignitaries and very influential people came to know him as they became his regular guests on his yacht. They admired this man with very humble beginnings. From a young immigrant family in his new country, he had emerged and had become a significant symbol proving that anyone who wanted to succeed could do so, no matter what his background.

The Sicilian mafia elite who, with time, had become great fans of his success; recognized the importance of Alfonzo becoming part of their fantastic family circle and were looking at opportunities as to how they could get a piece of his Dream Investments fortune. They already had their connections in Montreal as in many other key cities on many continents. They had a solid grip on anything that had to do with money. They had established a very sophisticated network throughout the world.

What they found interesting about Alfonzo's company is that while they would keep a tight grip on controlling what they currently had ongoing worldwide, they had become more and more interested in his way of doing business which did not involve drugs sales, money laundering, prostitutes and running strippers or anything that had to be done in business back rooms or basements.

His business model was executed flawlessly and in plain light. They liked this idealistic proposal of joining his way of operating his business as it would not give rise to any suspicions about them being involved. As they would fall under the cover of his umbrella, he had his reputation well anchored within the business community due to years of hard work; they would remain in the shadows while collecting huge amounts of money.

Alfonzo had never received any reproaches for his business method of operation; it was a very clean and ethical business.

Real Estate was a very hot commodity and he had purchased hundreds of condominium around the world, on the most exotic and exclusive locations. He had put his company on the stock exchange for investors, the returns were too good to be true but they were real. His company had the best stock exchange rates on the stock exchange. They were the envy of many other companies.

Many investors have achieved their pot of gold and new heights of wealth that no one else had ever reached in such a short amount of time.

Chapter 5

The first step in the making of a criminal

With time, the Sicilian mafia developed ties with Alfonzo. There were at first casual and friendly meetings on his yacht or theirs, enjoying very pricy Cuban cigars and cognacs. Other times, it was exclusive wine degustation in private villas situated in the picturesque mountains overlooking the Mediterranean Sea where some promiscuous activities had taken place.

They did not hold back in paying for privacy and exclusivity which allowed them highly paid horseback rides and excursions in the Madonie Park to Mount Etna. He had flown several times throughout the years to the UK from Sicilia to participate with the upper echelon on horse races as he had become the owner of several thoroughbreds. Other times became more subtle as they involved the testing a new type of cocaine on which he had become rapidly hooked.

He had over time been introduced to acquaintances and family members of his first contacts and after a while, one of his regular friends had attempted more than a few times to introduce him to his special other family leader but he had managed to decline these invitations. He strongly suspected that it could be a disguise in order to take over the control of his company. Alfonzo didn't know much about them but he knew enough about how the mafia could exert its influence to make its way inside his business.

He knew that on the first occasion he would overtly express his consent to meet them, it would be the point of no return and that he would never be able to get out of the trap for the rest of his life. He had to figure out a way to disconnect from them for good but he knew that it would not be easy.

He had this thought in the back of his head that if he were to continue on this path with this relationship, that he would soon lose total grip not only of his financial empire but on his life.

They wanted him to feel that he was now part of the great Sicilian family. After all, Alfonzo was of Sicilian descent. Membership in the "Cosa Nostra" was opened only to Sicilian men.

Alfonzo withdrew from them for a while and made his trips to Sicilia less regularly than before. He did his best to keep his vacation timing secret and was also making them purposely shorter than usual. He had managed to give all kinds of reasons why he couldn't make the trip or answer positively to their invitations.

He invented all kinds of justifications mainly regarding the market becoming fragile and that he needed to tightly supervise and understand the volatility and changes of the investment markets and address the concerns and uncertainties of some of his investors so as to not lose them.

No one from his company executive team or his parents knew that he had developed ties with the Sicilian mafia.

Alfonzo kept everything to himself. But it was already too late. Too many people knew about his social gatherings with them.

It had become a potential danger for his reputation, his client and investor's trust, etc. which could be used for blackmail and destroy what he had sweated for, his success and his irreproachable reputation.

With time, they finally had persuaded him that he needed protection since so much was now loosely left up for grabs by anyone out in the open and able to destroy his reputation. They laid out plans as to how his company could take over additional real estate markets and other investments throughout the world.

They wanted part of it in exchange for providing their connections influences, power and most importantly their protection from competition and theft for which they had an excellent reputation of addressing in a very forceful manner. All of the moneys coming from their illegal earnings activities would be funnelled into his investment company.

As their money transfers to his company would be entirely done illicitly so as to turn it into clean money, Alfonzo first didn't like the approach of shadow financing. It was not his way of doing business but he became completely won over, he had no choice; he gave way to their pressure.

The whole affair seemed to turn against him as he had tried to counter punch their approach in order to keep his company intact from their influence. He certainly knew however how much of the mafia's power had come from its reputation to commit violence, particularly murder, against virtually anyone. He certainly knew that he was no exception to their rules in terms of dealing with opponents.

He would certainly have a taste of what they would be able to inflict him if he tried to get out of their proposal. Part of the blackmail had been that they would take care of the family pizzeria business and it included the fate of his parents and other family members. They laid out some pictures and videos for him to see. The totality of his not so ethical secretly filmed gatherings with ladies would very easily make good headlines if he did not going along with their proposal. This was a complete set up to destroy his reputation and this became greatly terrifying to him.

Thinking it over for days, he had given his agreement under such duress and blackmail, they now had become integral partners of his company; he was panicking at the thought that if he'd reach for the authorities and reveal to them that he was completely at the mercy of criminals. Imagining what they would do to his family, he completely backed off from that idea. He knew at that point; even before beginning this new business partnership that he had lost. It was now impossible for him to back away from them.

Along with the new agreement, he had to give several pink sheets to his loyal executives and replace them with the mafia family members who would take care of the business as effectively, he was told, as their predecessors. He had never criticized his employees. They were irreproachable and the most loyal executives he could have ever hired.

The reasons he had given them were based on superficial reasons and he several times was challenged to give proof of what he was accusing them of doing.

What had played into his favour while firing his employees was that at the time the market had become unpredictably volatile for some months and that he had to make drastic changes if he didn't want to see the company shares plummet.

While he knew that what he had imposed on his staff was plainly wrong, and while he knew that he was destroying everything he had stood for within himself, his urge to survive had taken over his integrity. Alfonzo would soon become an unrecognizable man as he finally accepted to meet the mafia boss.

His employees knew that something fishy was going on but when they confronted him on the fact of what they strongly felt was taking place, Alfonzo always managed to deny it.

Chapter 6

Meeting with the mob boss

He had gained most of his knowledge of the mafia from the God father movies and some other shows such as the Sopranos TV series.

While Montreal was the second cradle of Sicilian mafia in the world, little did he know about the direct impact they had throughout the Little Italy neighbourhood in which he had grown up.

It had never crossed his mind that his parents might have been targets of the mafia or that it might even possibly be the case. Alfonzo had never seen or heard anything that could possibly have been a hint that it could possibly be the case.

The reason was very simple; the operating basis of the mafia in the city was very subtle and they ran in the shadows as best as they could. There was no intention to let anything come to light pertaining to their various drug, prostitution, construction contracting, building purchases and casino money laundering.

If his parents had become victims of the mafia, they had never told him. Their method of approaching potential clients, was aggressive but friendly, they labelled their work as being door-to-door salesmen looking out for the stores and restaurant's best interest for a little monthly percentage contribution from their net profit.

They would collect on time or sadness, desolation and violence such as Molotov cocktails would soon be exploding inside their businesses.

During one of his latest vacations where he had docked his yacht near the Cala Mosche beach at sun set, Alfonzo was expecting the mafia boss's message from which would fully inform him of the meeting details. He would meet them and find out a new structural business plan they had in mind for the newly rebranded Dream Investments Company.

Alfonzo was flown in a private jet from Catania Fontanarossa Airport to Aeroporto Vincenzo Florio where a Roll Royce waited for him near the tarmac where he landed. He was driven to Marsala, an Italian town located in the Province of Trapani in the westernmost part of Sicily. After a short drive out of the town, the car stopped before a high fence where the driver introduced himself to security with his guest.

As the gate opened, he was driven up to the half moon driveway to a huge villa. A man with a woman and three children were standing in the entrance of the house, obviously waiting for him. These were the people he was there to meet, the Di Salvo family.

All around them, were several heavily armed men which amazingly enough didn't seem to intimidate the family members who were watching him as he exited the car. It looked as if they were simple features added to the usual scenery. Alfonzo couldn't explain what he was seeing in any other way.

- Welcome to my summer home, Alfonzo. The man walked towards him and they shook hands. The man's grip was very firm. I am Paolo, he said. This is my wife, Marcella and my three children, Paolo Jr., Mario and Manuela. OK, kids, go play, please follow me, it will be better inside, the humidity is really too much today to enjoy the outdoors.

The kids didn't take long to respond and disappeared inside the house. His wife looked to be a very reserved type of person who Alfonzo felt made a great effort to produce a smile that was not really genuine while she shook his hand in a very weak fashion. He felt as if her hands had no bones.

Paolo invited Alfonzo to enter and signaled the driver to leave. He would not be needed for a few hours. The driver responded immediately and drove away on a narrowed road beside the villa.

This was no ordinary summer home, he could tell just by looking at everything around him. The place outside was surrounded by vineyards, a wonderful landscape standing overlooking the ocean.

There was a pool area featuring a solarium provided for sun loungers, overlooking the vineyards and a huge veranda which gave way to a flower garden. The place was impeccably maintained. As he entered the ground floor, he found himself in the living area, he felt that he had entered into a Mediterranean designed castle. Marcella was soon to excuse herself as she had some business to attend to and left the two men alone.

- Come with me Alfonzo, it will be more conformable to converse in my cigar room.

With the stone accents, hand-scraped wood flooring and Venetian plaster on the walls and ceiling, the room had the ultimate in finishes. The leather chairs and textured walls made this contemporary space look like an old-time cigar lounge in a gentleman's club. Alfonzo became more and more negatively impressed at the luxurious mansion as he became conscious of the tremendous amount of money it had taken to build it.

- Do you wish to have a drink?

As he gestured towards a huge bar with a great amount of wines, liquors, beers, vodkas, gins, whiskeys, rums, brandies and bourbons. The whole place had more varied choice of spirits than any of the bars he had ever attended.

I'll have bourbon, please.

Paolo Di Salvo had a very particular facial feature; a scarred line just under his left eye. Alfonzo was stricken by the look of this man. He tried his best to restrain himself from imagining the kind of duress he had been subjected to have inherited such a serious mark on his face. It was certainly not a birthmark.

Paolo immediately and very elegantly took a few ice cubes and placed them into a heavy bottomed crystal glass and poured bourbon. He just had handed him a Pappy Van Winkle's Family Reserve 20 Year old.

- Please, take a seat. I am glad that you have accepted my invitation. I have recently taken over the position as the head of the family as my uncle Alberto sadly died of a heart attack. He was a very loyal man to the family and I owe him a lot. My life wouldn't have been as blessed without his fatherly intervention.

Alfonzo was feeling as if he was melting into his chair; he was very nervous at the thought that this man was without any hesitation about to destroy his company.

- What is it that you exactly want? Asked Alfonzo who felt that he could possibly get out of this imposed merger offer.

- Well we have all come to the conclusion that you would be better off with our assistance and the combining of our efforts to guarantee you that you will remain strong and be the only multinational corporation; the one that will outlive any other similar business in the world.

Alfonzo was squeezing his glass in his right hand; he was fuming inside his head at what he had just heard. The glass suddenly shattered into pieces. The bourbon dripped onto the leather armchair. Alfonzo stood up and using his handkerchief from his pocket wiped the chair as best as he could.

- Do not worry about this, insisted Paolo. It is just a little accident. I'll get my maid to come and do the clean-up. He pressed a button situated near the wooded outline of the fireplace and a maid hurried in, arriving in the room in less than 20 seconds and immediately started the clean up as he indicated to her where the mess had occurred. She quickly cleaned the chair, using a spray cleaner and swept the floor with a little broom and in no time disappeared as fast as she appeared.

Alfonzo had wished that he was thousands miles away from the godfather. He couldn't figure a way out. He certainly didn't want to see his parents involved in the situation and until he could figure out how to get out of this situation, he had to play the game Paolo's way so they would not be placed into any danger.

Alfonzo then was invited to sit down again with another double bourbon in a new glass and to listen very carefully to what Paolo had to tell him. He wanted to make sure that he understood that what he was about to know about his family be respectfully listened to.

Their clan hierarchy was composed of Paolo Di Salvo, the father of them all. He was actually surprising enough the same age as Alfonzo. He had a family of his own, three kids and his wife who had been for several years, until she married Paolo, a very popular Italian actress.

At first Alfonzo thought they looked like a very ordinary family but the more the discussion evolved, he discovered a morbid side, the real Mafioso side. He now understood Paolo's wife's facial expression. She was probably terrified of this man.

Paolo described to him what the family business was all about: Their hierarchy, the initiation ceremony that he would soon attend, what the etiquette within the business, the meaning of Omertà, the code of silence that had to be respected as the penalty for its transgression was death. He went on to describe the whole client relations he had with the business in which they were involved, how they protected territories, depending on the type of activities within them.

He paused for a few seconds, time to wet the inside of his mouth with his bourbon.

- You know, Alfonzo, that you are very lucky to be part of the family. You do not have relative in the police and you have good moral values. This is why so many have been attracted to you as a man and a business man. You are a single man, this is however not too difficult to understand. But one day, you will find your match and will be able to build your own family where every one of your descendents will be proud of your accomplishments.

It will of course be necessary for you to marry a Sicilian. But this is not the priority right now. While it is still very important, I want to establish with you our way of working. You will find that our network is very sophisticated and efficient. We have invested a lot of money in order to have a flawless and very complex I.T. communication system, our multiple servers mostly run wirelessly and this cloud computing allows us to access information anywhere using any device compatible with our systems. We are capable of knowing what is happening in our business anywhere on the planet within a manner of minutes. Everything is of course exchanged in encrypted or cipher texted information which makes it impossible to be cracked by outsiders.

At a press of a button, a TV screen moved up from the bottom of the wall and Paolo presented to him the whole state of his affairs, his businesses network throughout the world.

Graphics were moving up and down the boards per categories such as: International and individual country monetary gross collections from each type of their transactions. The board was very impressive. Paolo went into more details as a switch of a button showed him the wealth of his empire, the successful operations base that his father had structured and built just before his death.

The entire operation was very elaborate; it included several investors and the money kept pouring in, they were operating in total safety under a flag of goodwill and sharing their wealth under several pseudonyms for cover purposes.

Their control over the construction contracts, both public and private had resulted in billions and the crushing of their competitors. Violence and vandalism were their last recourses and they never wanted to use them if not necessary.

The same operating basis was also in place for the loan sharking. Their interest rates were phenomenal and for someone to deal with this had to have strong nerves while being desperate to borrow from them.

While there had always been casualties along the way, inevitably due to their last recourse in certain circumstances, their dirty work had always been executed by the lowest echelon of connections who were never informed as to who they were working for; they were mainly muscle, professional killers and snipers.

Paolo or anyone belonging to his network never employed locals to do the job. They were instead vacationers who came for a visit, lounging in luxurious hotels, enjoying the beaches until the time was right to flawlessly perform their dirty jobs.

They could be the unlikely grand-ma' or grand-pa' who happened to be ex-convicts willing to risk anything for a quick and very lucrative reward. The choice of the individuals and their ages always depended on the type of targeting. They were always contacted by a third party. It was an expensive operation and effortlessly carried out.

Alfonso strongly suspected that they had a very bad reputation for violence but Paolo insisted that this was a thing of the past and that they now used a softer approach in their dealings. They used to get rid of people but as they had taken over the power of several underground branches of trafficking, the need for exterminating people who were a menace had pretty much disappeared or these individuals joined them, being too fearful to confront anyone in the family or whoever they were using to clearly make their point.

Their fearsome reputation had gained strength through convincing verbal intimidation and it had worked.

After several hours of discussion and agreement, Alfonzo had finalized the rules under which he would from now on operate and was ready to leave the villa; he would have 10 billion American dollars wired to him, to be deposited in his bank account the next day. A business deal had been reached.

Alfonzo would remain the CEO and President of the company in theory, nothing would ever change regarding this, but the power and distribution of power would be originating from another source. He would be the one to report to the boss and be accountable for all the financial transactions, purchases, etc.

Once he would gain the approval of the boss, he would be free to run his affairs as he wished. These were the conditions, the most important ones in the eyes of Paolo Di Salvo.

Chapter 7

Martina Di Salvo

Since their association with the Sicilian mafia boss and his workforce, Dream Investments' stocks had ballooned to new heights. With this new alliance, it didn't take long for Alfonzo to observe the crushing of competitive investment groups watching them take deep dives from which they would either suffer great pain while attempting to crawl out of the mess at a snail's pace while trying to regain strength or file for bankruptcy.

They mercilessly crushed any other investment firm competition, cutting the number of competitors to an all time low.
Some of the companies under attack were not about to give up and hired private investigators who specialized in tracking down the original sources of their attacks by following the financial trend patterns that made investors switch gears and transfer their investments over to Dream Investments.

The pattern was too obvious to be ignored. But what was more importantly challenging was to find out what had created such havoc towards them in such a short amount of time. This would come back on Alfonzo with a vengeance.

Life was good for Alfonzo and everyone at Dream Investments. He soon put aside his fears that he would go to Hell as he realised that his celebrity status had reached the peak of fame and attention. He was the top financier mogul reigning over the international market.

To commemorate their first year of success, the location for the celebration had been set in the city of Syracuse at a private 5 star club where the view of the Mediterranean Sea was breathtaking. Only the elite and new investors were invited to celebrate the company's achievements.

This is where Alfonzo met the love of his life. Her name was Martina. A very impressive woman not only physically but also by the way she would look at a man kind of challenging him daring him to think that women were inferior to men.

She was a tall woman and who had the look and presence of Uma Thurman, the American actress who had performed leading roles in a variety of films, ranging from romantic comedies and dramas to science fiction and action movies. Paolo introduced his beautiful cousin to Alfonzo right after their luxury four course dinner.

Paolo made his rounds to greet his guests accompanied by a woman that Alfonzo had never met before.

- My cousin, Martina, Martina, this is Alfonzo, our business partner. Alfonzo stood up right away, impressed by this amazingly elegant blond beauty.

She wore a white Dolce & Gabbana dress, showing off her curves with ease in a corset gown.

Cupid, the son of the love goddess Venus hit Alfonzo's heart!
- Pleased to meet you Martina, would you mind accompanying me to the bar, I'd like to offer you a drink. Alfonzo was all eyes on her. Couldn't imagine how he could manage to stay away from her. His alpha male instinct fired up and he had to find a way to court her long enough in order to charm her and make her fall for him.

Paolo excused himself from their presence, satisfied that the contact was finally made and hoped that his cousin would score big with him. It was important that everything including business stay within the family.

With Paolo's assistance, Martina had been freed from a union that had gone bad. She had married one of the Sicilian mob members who had treated her very poorly.

She had been confined within the walls of a house where she had not been allowed any freedom after only a few months of being married. Paolo got her out of the mess. Her husband's jealousy mixed with his drug addiction transformed him into a monster who abused her physically and psychologically. He had repeatedly raped her and angrily beaten her regularly for no reason.

Paolo witnessed the brutality of this man having once arrived at the hospital where he saw firsthand a heavily disfigured Martina; she was unrecognizable. She had been found lying unconscious on the bathroom floor of her house. She had undergone several plastic surgeries that he had generously financed.

It was said that not long after this latest episode of cruelty towards his wife that her then husband had mysteriously disappeared while on a business trip overseas; his body had never been found.
- What will it be for you miss? Asked a bar tender.

- It will be a Fernet-Branca on ice.

- And for you Sir?

- An Amaretto on ice with spring water on the side.

As the bar tender got busy pouring their drinks, Martina touched his red rose so as to properly adjust it.

- Nice rose that you have. So, how long have you been with the family?

- A year or so and so far, I have to say that I really like the ride.

- You should not be so quick in your thinking; it doesn't mean that it will remain as smooth a ride as you might believe. I've been in this family long enough to say that in this type of business, you've got a lot to lose if you do not walk the walk and talk the talk you are forced to obey. But I guess, I am like you, I am trapped with these demons and I have no way out.

Alfonzo was very surprised at her outspoken way of describing the style of life she appeared to be living. Was she someone Paolo sent to him to try him and find out his true intention? Was he really being honest towards them or was he covertly disaffected?

It didn't take long before he realised that she was not a plant. They saw each other regularly and took vacations together; their favorite time was to go to the Alps and enjoy skiing together or cruising aboard his yacht on the Mediterranean.

With time, he proposed to her and she happily accepted. Paolo was delighted with the news and he personally took care of planning their wedding, the guest lists, location, etc. etc. He wanted it to be a very special occasion which would increase the ties within the notorious family.

The wedding took place on a beautiful summer day at the Notre-Dame Basilica of Montreal, the most significant part of the Catholic religious heritage of the city.

Both looked like members of royalty from an unknown but certainly rich kingdom. As the bells rang signaling that the private but very crowded church ceremony had reached its end, the media were all over covering the event and impatiently waiting to see the couple emerge from the church. This couldn't be averted.

He was too well known. He was a celebrity. The couple made their exit with a tremendous amount of rose petals being thrown at them. It was a great day for both of them. They had pledged to each other to make their lives a special loving journey.

Alfonzo was the happiest man in the world. Martina brought him something that he had not felt ever before. He had found in her what he was missing. Someone with whom he could share his feelings and allowed him to be himself which enabled him to turn away from what he had endured for a long time, a life alone.

He bought a luxurious penthouse which had a breathtaking panoramic view of the city including Mont Royal, the St-Lawrence River and the South Shore of the city. Martina would have to get used to winter, which she didn't really mind. Being with him was all that counted.

Chapter 8

The perfect love and business union

It didn't take long for Martina to get in the groove and participate in several of the schemes Alfonzo had developed over the years. While the money was more than good, the needing to create more income had become a very stressful situation resting solely on their shoulders.

The demand for increasing percentages of the profit had become out of proportion, Paolo profiting tremendously from his influence over Alfonzo's wife was able to get her to do anything possible in order to respond to his demands. She soon understood that in order to keep Alfonzo afloat in this dreadful situation that she had to participate and inevitably share the burden.

As Alfonzo introduced his wife to several of his investors and clients, she gained enough of their trust and had successfully learned how to forge the female investor's signatures, gather personal information and create false IDs in order for her to enter in any bank in the country or elsewhere to make changes in their investments and even cash their capital under their names. The purpose was to invest it all back in to the stock markets. It was just a courteously to assist them by making investments for them.

This is what Alfonzo had been doing for a while for the male side of the business.

All the while, they would send fat checks regularly to their investors with their returns «according to the performance of the stock, while holding their capital that had remained untouched."

Nobody had ever suspected anything wrong; they were both such a loving couple and were particularly very dedicated to the older men they happened to invite to their yacht for a once in a lifetime private luxurious cruises. The charming ammo used to invest in the Dream Investments worked its magic every time.

Everything was set up to seduce rich old men coming from several countries across Europe, the Middle-East, the USA, South America and Canada to invest their money in Dream Investments. The special cruises included private striptease shows, prostitutes of their choice.

Martina did her best to provide what her clients wanted, dealing with a Philippine underground human trafficking network. The whole scheme concerning the yacht's favors was engineered to get these men separated from their money in exchange of their secretive and promiscuous journey aboard the yacht. They liked it so much that many of them made these trips several times a year to the Mediterranean Sea.

Basically, the operation emptied their pockets and they all lied to their spouses, who had felt that they had bizarrely not been invited. It was positioned as being a new men's club where Dream Investments would gather them on the yacht and they would be rewarded for their trust in the company.

Their coffers emptied proportionally to the amount of pleasures offered. As blackmail was used to get more money, they too were caught up in a very vicious circle form which they couldn't make their way out. Martina became overwhelmed by the abundance coming their way. It had become a very lucrative activity.

They successfully accrued investment bonds, grandchildren's scholarship investments, overseas real estate; stocks and bonds, deeds for their retirement homes and condos and lots of cash. The cheques, etc. kept coming.

There was nothing they couldn't put their hands on as these men had become birds eating out of their hands not because of trust but because of the scandalous revelations they faced should they act otherwise. The stakes were too high.

The loving couple didn't care if this could ruin their lives. Their own lives would be ruined if they didn't come up with the cash Paolo was claiming they owed to him.

"Where there is money, there is a way to access it!" had become Alfonzo and Martina's motto. Both were taking great risks but as long as they could continue to spin the money sufficiently enough, they had hoped that one day, they could make above and beyond the expected amounts to eventually stop their abberated pattern of operation and return to a normal life within a few months.

While they felt that while they gave way more to him from the money they had generated than he deserved, greedy Paolo had become a hungry monster and just kept demanding more.

Chapter 9

The 's..t' hit the fan

They had always sincerely hoped that the situation would end with no more casualties than necessary but the shit hit the fan soon after as one of the men who had taken the trips to the yacht as a regular, literally became the first fatality of the business.

He was found dead floating in the middle of the yacht's Jacuzzi only visible under the light of the moon in the middle of the night. It was the nightshift chef who happened to go out on the deck for a cigarette break who made the gruesome discovery of a non responsive man in the water.

He immediately alerted Alfonzo who was sitting in his living room watching a movie with Martina. They jumped out of their love seat and ran up to the deck. They couldn't believe their eyes.

As Martina sat at one table trying to figure out what to do next, she found a suicide note on the table under an a half full Champaign flute where the man had written in an unsteady hand that life was not worth living since he had become involved in Dream Investments, that it had ruined his life.

He couldn't stand before his wife, his children and grand-children and confess everything regarding his promiscuity and the fact that he had become a drug addict. He was a very renowned retired Swiss German banker. He had literally given away his fortune to Dream Investments.

They couldn't get rid of the body as this would immediately ignite suspicions of possible foul play. Alfonzo had become very upset to see this unfolding before him. Never in his life had he ever though that he would witness a scene of suicide.

Martina contacted her cousin for his expertise on how to deal with the situation. She used specific communication codes so that he knew exactly what she was dealing with. He gave her the information she needed in order to deal with the Sicilian authorities while covering the Dream Investments activities aboard the yacht.

The captain of the ship made a 180 degree turn around of the yacht's position in order for the entertainment personnel to quickly gather their belongings and run half naked to board a small ship which brought them ashore where a limousine drove them away from the scene. It had been performed so rapidly that it had been impossible for them to see the body still floating on the other side.

Martina made sure that only the scattered running lights remained activated until the cops arrived at the yacht. The cops and investigators showed up within an hour following Martina's call. The suicide note was burned to cinder; Martina crushed it into finer power using a mortar and pestle to make sure that there was no possible traceable residue anywhere before flushing it down the toilet.

As the suicide note had been hidden fast enough so as to make sure that no one other than Martina an Alfonzo had read it, nobody else knew what had really happened. The other guests had been sleeping in their rooms and everything outside was very quiet.

The sirens were heard as the police boats approached the yacht which woke everyone. The yacht guests appeared one after the other on the deck in nightgowns wondering what could possibly have happened. They soon realised that none of their entertainers were aboard and now they were finding themselves watching cops taking pictures of the poor man floating in the Jacuzzi, others were looking for hand prints, etc.

They were all frightened by the scene and more concerned as to what they would have to tell the cops and try their best to cover up the very reasons why they were aboard. They didn't want to have anything to do with publicizing their presence on the yacht or regarding their 'personal pleasure business' making the news back in their home countries.

As they were all standing there nervously watching the situation, the two of the yacht's maids rapidly made their rounds through every guest room to gather any suspicious items that could have been left behind by the men and women who had earlier entertained their visitors. It was imperative that they protect their guests.

They were promised that if they were doing a good job that they would get a fat brown envelop in return. The men who left their rooms were not aware of what had just taken place. The sweeping took no time and they reported to Martina that everything was back in order.

- Have you found any interesting stuff, she asked.

- Well, Maam, said Imie one of her maids, she was kind of withholding laughing out loud, well, we found some... things and we did a good clean up...

She accompanied the maids and verified herself that it was the case.
- OK, show me what you have found.

She guided her to the galley and indicated to her where they had thrown in the shredder all the bras and fancy underwear they had found. Fortunately, the shredder also gave way down the drain to the ocean. There were a few empty bottles that they had put in the recuperation bins.

Both maids did a good job. Martina gave a sigh of relief and profusely thanked them for their good work. The award would be delivered the next day and they could now retire for the night.

One police man happened to enter in the galley as the maids were leaving and saw Martina standing in front of the sink crying with relief that she had pulled this off. She was a woman who was ready to do anything to save her way of living, the life of her husband and everything that that had to do with her union with the man she loved.

- Maam, you're OK?

- No, I am not, she cried, waving her hands close to her face as a sign that she was looking for her breath. How can something like this happen? I am so upset! I do not know what to say. I knew this man very well; he was a great respected man and business partner. He didn't deserve to die!

- Come with me, I have a few questions for you.

She joined Alfonzo who was already undergoing questioning by the cops. He was in the company of his chef who was also giving his testimony.

Chapter 10

The after shock

It was a long sleepless night for everyone aboard. The investigation took a long time; interrogating everyone on the yacht without exception before they could assert that there was nothing they had found on the yacht associated with violence or anything which would indicate an inflicted or forced drowning of the man.

The man's body was taken out of the water, put into a black body bag and transported to the coroner for further examination and as the police left, they were 100% sure that this was an accident, it seemed that the man had drunk quite a lot of alcohol which could have played a major role in his death.

Unless something could be found to contradict what they had observed thus far, they had positively concluded that the cause of his death was an unfortunate accident.

The guests played their role as being retired men on vacation who came for a break to breathe fresh air in a quiet place; that they were Dream Investments senior financial investors, it was part of their benefits that they be rewarded with free cruises as a bonus for their investment in and commitment to the company.

None of them was ever to be seen again on the yacht; too much was already at stake for them and their reputations. Upon their departure, they would however be dragged down by Martina and Alfonzo's blackmail as despite the distance, this would certainly not be cut out.

So, the money would still flow without encountering any resistance. Amazingly, the media was muzzled before anything could get out into the newspapers, online or on local TV. Nothing was ever published about the death on the Dream Investments' yacht.

Paolo was certainly behind addressing the scene to protect his interests. He was surprisingly, in the eyes of many who happened to know him, very effective in everything he was doing. Unknown by all, he was the sole owner of all the media on the island and throughout most of Italy.

The police closed the case as being accidental and did not file charges on anybody who had witnessed the scene. Brown envelops soon followed at the police H.Q. and the coroner and everyone went back to business as usual.

The man's body had been flown to Switzerland and picked up by his family for his funerals. A letter from the coroner accompanied the body informing them of the examination and the cause of his death. It was an accidental drowning due to an unfortunate cardiac arrest. The man already had a story of medical issues and had once gone under the scalpel for a by-pass heart surgery.

Everything about this incident had been swept clean. As they found themselves now alone with their crew, Martina and Alfonzo had to double their security as they were not sure if the family of this man would just take the coroner's information for granted and move on with their lives or try to do something else which could certainly include the running of their own investigation.

While they felt that they had not committed anything illegal relating to the death of the man, nothing could guarantee that the man's family would be quiet about it. They didn't know his family members well enough to be 100% sure that there would not be any reaction from them when they might soon have questions regarding the circumstances of his death.

As a gesture of showing genuine sympathy to his family members, Paolo arranged that they receive flowers and condolences offered to the family for his funeral. The message read that they were saddened to have lost a genuine professional friend and that he would be greatly missed by the Dream Investments family.

They hoped that their condolences would be well accepted and considered as genuine.

Chapter 11

A mandatory "family meeting"

One of the advantages of Dream Investments was that Alfonzo and Martina could operate and manage their company from anywhere in the world as most of its operation was done in the cyber world using very sophisticated software which Paolo, Martina along with his new executives had helped to set up.

The groundwork was done by "subcontractors'' who were so far away down the line , they had no cyber connection with the real administrators of Dream Investments. They didn't know by name any of the people for whom they worked or who was paying them; the pyramidal ladder was so huge that not one of them would ever find out who exactly was behind their income, their investment returns, even when retiring. This was the era of a very modern way of doing business; the more unrefined ways of contacts were made, the better it protected their covert activity.

All they knew was that the jobs were good and well paying and that they never had to wait for their payments. When the job was done, they were swiftly paid no questions asked.

While it was still a very lucrative business operation even minus the yacht activities, Paolo, sent an encrypted message to Martina and Alfonzo which meant that a mandatory meeting had to be held ASAP at Paolo's summer villa.

There was no time limit when to reply in the message, it was clear that they had to act immediately and show up as he had ordered them to do. The transport arrangements were already set for them. All they had to do was to pack up and go.

The trip to Marsala seemed longer than usual. They knew that they would be in trouble if everything was blown out of the water. While Alfonzo or Martina certainly had an idea as to the reason he wanted to meet them, they knew that they would be more than reprimanded for the situation.

On arrival, the fences finally opened, there was only Paolo standing in front of the villa, smoking a cigar obviously waiting for them. As they got out the limousine, it drove away on the path beside the villa. His wife and kids were nowhere to be seen. It seemed that they had left the place as it was late in the fall.

- Hey Paolo!

- Hey Martina, said Paolo, kissing her cheeks.

As he was sort of welcomed Martina there was not very much a greeting of any sort towards Alfonzo. He took a serious look at them and invited them to follow him inside the house.

- Come with me, I have to go over something very important with you.

They soon joined him in his living room and offered them a drink. Alfonzo refused the offer while Martina requested spring water. The longer they were in Paolo presence; the more they felt that they would be lucky if they were to ever get out of his villa alive and in one piece.

After pouring himself a drink, Paolo remained standing up before them and expressed his anger towards them.

- You fuckers! Shit heads! I paid the media! I paid the cops! I paid the coroner! I paid millions of Euros to save your asses!

- Listen Paolo, Martina who began to implore him to listen to what she intended to say.

- Shut up bitch!

Alfonzo couldn't stand him calling his wife such a disgusting name.

- Don't ever treat my wife like this, Paolo. Let's have an adult conversation here.

- Shut up! You too bastard! You have no say and nothing can justify what happened on the yacht! You have dirtied the reputation of our business. What do you think will happen in Switzerland when they pick up the man's body at the morgue? Do you think that everything will go quietly from there? I did my best to shut down everything within my influence but my arms are not long enough to influence what might be stirring inside his family's heads.

I'll have to deal with that situation myself and go there to make damage control. It won't be easy but I have to do it. Martina, what have you done? Was this an idea of yours to transform the yacht into a bordello? Or was it you, Alfonzo who came up with the idea?

- It's me, Paolo, said Martina. I did it as I knew that if I were to bring the best incentives in the business that these men would pay. We had no choice; you have taken us by the throat with your percentage increases. We had no other choice other than to improvise new things in order to pay. It's your fault; we did not have the choice! She screamed at him.

He approached her and slapped her in the face.

- You bitch, how you dare say that to me! You are the one who is ungrateful. I got you out of the shit you were in before you met Alfonzo!

Alfonzo started to fight with him, grabbing him by the arm and told him to never lift his finger against his wife again. This is when they both engaged in a physical fight, grabbing anything close at hand and using these to inflict as much as pain they could, ending up with deep cuts and bruises on their faces which bled proficiently.

Martina finally succeed in separating them, pulling Alfonzo from Paolo's grip.

- Stop it both of you; this is not the way to address the matter! I have a better way!

As they both used their handkerchiefs to wipe the blood off their faces, they didn't exchange any words. They were just looking at the state of their physical condition.

She dragged them, one by one and pushed them toward the leather chairs, handled them some water and told them to sit and listen to what she had to say.

- I never expected this suicide incident to happen on the yacht; that you dared label me as a bitch when I tried my best to cover everything up regarding our activities is disgusting, Paolo! You have no idea as to what it took for us to save face before these cops, who scrutinized every one and the whole yacht!. They took their time; it took an eternity before they finally left with the dead man! They remained on the yacht for hours, Paolo, hours! You do not know what it took for us to save our asses and by the way, in case you have not realised it yet, it includes yours!!! Do you think that we were happy to see this dead old man floating on the water? How can you dare say that? I am disgusted!

- Paolo, I am leaving and I am disconnecting from everything that has to do with you and the rest of the operation. I am quitting Paolo! I am disgusted and I cannot stand this anymore. You've gone too far, way too far, you have poisoned our lives and we were so desperate that we have taken awkward solutions to pay you, you my cousin! You, ungrateful bastard that you are! I deny belonging to the same blood line as yours! You have enriched yourself and pocketed huge amounts of money because of us!

- Alfonzo, let's leave him here in this mess as it suits him so well. Maybe he will come back to his senses and realise what he is doing but I doubt it very much. I know him too well. He has no respect for our family – The very first commitment he swore to make was to protect his family as the upmost importance when he took his oath for the top job! I know you did this Paolo; I was there when you said these words! Remember? And no, I do not owe you anything anymore Paolo. You are a disgusting piece of shit! I have had it! She took a Chrystal candle holder that was standing over the fireplace and threw it at one of the walls and screamed at him: You are the most perverted mind I have ever met! Arrivederci Porco Dio!

She walked out the villa completely shaken up, crying and swearing. Her white dress was completely stained with blood and she didn't give a damn as to how she looked as she went searching for the limousine driver who had parked the car behind the villa.

Alfonzo was soon to follow her, walking awkwardly, limping his way out. He didn't say anything to Paolo, didn't bother to look at him. Paolo who was still sitting on his chair, wiping his face surrounded by pieces of high priced now ruined furniture and shattered crystal on the stained carpet. The violence exerted by the two men was unquestionable.

They were driven away while Paolo was still sitting, thinking over what to do next. He had just lost his best employees. As he knew Martina very well, he realised that he might have gone too far with her as she would never go back on her words or her decision.

He knew that she would not let Alfonzo to carry on either. He didn't mind that she parted ways with him but losing Alfonzo was not something the he could contemplate happening any time soon, it was not a possible option.

Alfonzo and Martina packed up and left the yacht the next day. They did their best with their maid's assistance to cover up Alfonzo bruises. They flew back to Montreal. They had to take action in order to erase everything related to their connection to the Sicilia mafia. They made the decision to sell the yacht as they didn't intend to ever return to Sicily. They were sure that it would sell in no time. It was one of a kind.

Leaving everything behind would not be an easy task. They were so involved in the business operation, it didn't matter how long they had performed as a team, their connections were the best in the market and the reason they had been able to shut down any competition throughout the world.

Dream Investments would lose all the precious connections that were so influential in keeping the rise of their stocks but at this point, Alfonzo and Martina didn't care. They did their best to save what was left of a company that had the greatest investment return rates in the international market. They knew that they would take a hit but at this point, they didn't give a damn.

They kept busy at transferring their moneys into new bank accounts, closing down old ones, leaving no traces of prior transaction records anywhere, abundantly paying knowledgeable bankers to make the changes and make everything completely legal. Paolo was soon to realise that he didn't have anything coming in from his due collections or being wired directly to his oversea bank accounts regularly as before.

What Martina and Alfonzo were not aware of, was that soon after they had left Sicily, Paolo had managed to contact the Swiss man family members and sent one of his lawyers to meet with them. As a gesture of "compassion", his lawyer handed them a 100$M Euros to the man's widow who had lost everything due to the tragic death of the retired banker.

It was three times the amount this man had invested in Dream Investments. He had made a point by telling them that he didn't wish to get Dream Investments' reputation being dirtied by unfounded suspicions and that he wished that they would keep their silence for the rest of their lives. At the reception of such amount of money, they signed the required papers, certifying before this very renowned lawyer that they would never make any attempt to sue or take any civil actions against Dream Investments or their investors.
The case was finally closed for good.

Chapter 12

A sour Christmas day

Back from their trip to Sicily, Alfonzo and Martina recognized that they were now living in a merciless world. They plunged into alcohol and cocaine use had become a daily fix they couldn't live without in order to deal with this stressful life.

During a Christmas holiday at their restaurant, Alfonzo's parents held an early family dinner. The restaurant was exceptionally closed for the occasion and would open at a later time. After the meal and the musical entertainment that they enjoyed very much, Alessandro, Alfonzo's father took him aside at the back of the kitchen, in a small room that he used for his accounting and began to slap his son across the face without telling him anything.

He was obviously furious at his son and the way he now physically looked. He knew something wrong has happening to him, his physical appearance was only one of the symptoms of what was really going on with him; it was something that he had prayed would never happen to his son. But now, looking at his son, what he had feared the most had already happened. He then screamed at him.

- What happened to you son? What is happening to you? Don't lie to me. I know what is going on. I always wanted to save you from them since you were born. They have given me and your mother the help we needed to get where we are now but you didn't have to do this! We have lived through hell because of them, why did you do this?

His father kept slapping him in the face, completely revolted that his son had put himself under the same duress that his family had been enduring since they had put their feet on their new country's soil.

- Why are you so mad at me when you are just telling me that you've just done the same thing?

- You didn't need to do this, you idiot! We wanted to save you from them and what do I find out? You have fired your best employees from the company, I know all about it and I know that there is only one reason why you have done this!

He then ripped Alfonzo's red rose from his suit and threw it toward one of the walls.

- You've sold your soul to them! To these bastardos!

He then took his son in his arms and cried loudly, screaming what have they done to you? What have they done to you? My son! My son! I am so sorry! So sorry!

He was screaming so loud, that everyone became silent inside the restaurant, hearing everything his father was saying. The waiters made an effort to make as much noise as they could with the plates and utensils in an effort to cover what was unfolding in the back office. The people assembled for the diner couldn't figure out what was going on.

Alfonzo's mother, Elena, turned on the music and increased the volume to signal to the waiters to get back to doing what they were supposed to be doing, as they needed to clean since the dinner was almost over. Clients were waiting outside to get in.

- I did it for the same reason you have done it, father.

- Don't tell me that they had threatened you! Is this what they had told you they would do? Son, tell me everything!

Alessandro and Elena had been observing their son and his wife for quite a while and had soon suspected that they might have become additional victims. He had all the indications of what his own parents had felt at the time, they had become less and less relaxed, often looking at who could be in the area watching them, the fact that they couldn't withdraw from the influence of the underground iron fist was making their lives miserable.

No one could however have guessed that this is what they were feeling on a daily basis.

It became clearer to him as he asked his father why he would not take his retirement as he could give his parents the money so they could very easily do it and be more than comfortable.

His father had wished that he could tell him that he was at the mercy of the mafia but his head was on the chopping board and they were so terrified about the outcome if he left the restaurant, that they might find their only child dead somewhere in the Montreal dark back alleys.

Martina joined them and they embraced each other crying in despair and so saddened by the frightening disclosure that had unfolded.

Chapter 13

Time to leave the past behind and start anew

The business would still run without any major glitches for a while until a suitable buyer was found, they hoped. Martina and Alfonzo decided to get away for a while, get away from everything that they felt had crucified them under what had seemed an endless duress.

They'd had quite enough of the intimidation, threats, blackmail, etc. They couldn't live like this anymore. After a few days of reflection, they made their move.

They paid a visit to the IL Sicilian pizzeria restaurant where Alfonzo wanted to have a long and straight talk with his parents and inform them where he exactly stood regarding the situation. His parents empathised with him knowing well how much he had struggled with alcohol and drugs and that he and Martina needed to get back on the right path. They assured him that he could go on and get a new and better life, build a family and finally be happy. There was nothing more his parents wished for both of them.

Alfonzo couldn't tell them when they would meet again but asserted that they would be protected. He had loyal friends that would definitely keep an eye on them to make sure that their restaurant would be kept secure until they closed it down and left the city. He emphasized that they too had no choice and that he cared about their safety. Handing him false ID passports, he added that his father and mother should retire and leave the city for their safety as soon as possible.

They agreed after such convincing arguments, he told them everything that had happened at the yacht and their confrontation with Paolo. They were definitely at risk. Alfonzo recommended that they move out west to Vancouver Island where there were well established Italian-Canadian organizations into which they could blend and enjoy this new environment.

Alfonzo and Martina stayed in Montreal until the day they went to the Airport to say their goodbyes to his parents. It was a very sad day as they were parting and they had no way of knowing when they would ever see each other again. But they hoped that they would reunite under a sun of liberty and contentment. It was heartbreaking to see his elderly parents going through such a hard time because of the path they had chosen to take. But they needed a break from everything the same way he needed one.

The day his father put the sign in the restaurant door window that he was closing down was a very emotional moment. Nobody in the neighborhood had expected this to happen so suddenly. Alessandro and Elena Pinocchia had worked very hard to make this place so memorable. So many memories were going to be left behind.

But it was necessary to turn the page and start anew. They had stashed enough cash from the rapid auction of everything that their restaurant owned, there were a few things left behind. Despite all the efforts to get it well boarded up, a few months later, it had been vandalized and occupied by homeless people and drug addicts until eventually a five alarm fire completely wiped it out.

All that was left of this family business was a part of the burned sign of the very popular IL Sicilian that had been hanging above the entrance that had withstood against winds and weather for so many years.

Then, it had become their turn to hand over the keys of their condo and they fled the country by private jet. They arrived a few days later at their new home; the Ariara Island in the Philippines. Just a few hours away from Hong Kong, where Alfonzo would be able to travel easily for business purposes, it was the ideal place and a few weeks later, he had managed to buy part of the island, making it harder to reach for anyone who would want to do harm to him or his wife. He hired heavily armed guards and the place was under surveillance 24/7. His loyal employees, his chefs, maids etc, who used to work for him at the yacht were flown to the island, happy to rejoin him.

Everything they had done to reach their new destination had been done under new identifications and names. Their passports were also under new IDs. Nobody could trace them. They in survival mode and nothing, not money or anything else would stop them from reaching their goals of having a quiet place where they could live in peace.

They also envisioned selling the business which would utterly get them completely unshackled from Paolo Di Salvo. As they looked at this possibility, it became the ultimate solution.

A month later, they put the business on the market to be sold. The stocks prices were holding high and it was the right time to sell. The amount of reaches was completely unbelievable; they would make a lot of cash and be able to have a life without hassles. They were looking at extending their family, having kids and living happily ever after with the proceeds of the sale of the business.

The news about Dream Investments had reached an unforgiving man. Paolo was very quickly informed that the Dream Investment's Company was for sale. That literally outraged him and he swore to himself that he had to become persuasive enough to get Alfonzo to back off from contemplating selling his company. His association with Alfonzo had been very costly to him and it was time for retribution.

Chapter 14

Adding ammo for self-protection

A year had passed without anything but good times, enjoying the good weather while always keeping an eye on their backs wherever they went. There was never any guarantee that they would not encounter problems along the way.

Alfonzo and Martina knew that the world could become a very small place at a second's notice. But since they had successfully sold the company, there was much less to be concerned about.

They both had managed to adapt to this stress less life and it was welcome. They didn't have to look for more unusual solutions; no worries except what would be served for dinner. Quite a change from what they had been dealing for years under Paolo's crushing demands. They involved themselves in various charity groups and contributed to their new community while keeping themselves from further engagements which could jeopardize their cover.

They soon realised however that the number of armed guards around their property was pulling in curiosity despite of all their efforts to make it known that they were entirely paying these guards for their protection and to avoid vandalism of their property. But it had definitely become an issue.

In order to diminish this growing curiosity from people that had developed overtime, Martina and Alfonzo hired a private martial arts teacher who trained them, which increased their confidence and strength. They felt that it was necessary in case of something happening which would put them in a position where they would need to know what to do and how to defend themselves. After tremendous effort, they soon became 3rd Dan black belts in judo.

In addition to these courses, while Martina and Alfonzo had never used a gun, they knew that this was the way to go. They hired an instructor for firearms safety courses, bought two American guns Colt 1911 Government Delta Elite 10mm's from a licenced gun dealer from Hong Kong. With their training under their belts, they felt confident that they would be able to face anything that might come their way.

After six months of absolute silence, Martina and Alfonzo finally managed to communicate with his parents who were delighted to know that they were doing well. Everything out west was fine with his parents. They had purchased a condo situated at the top of a hill on the west coast of Vancouver Island. The Pacific Ocean on one side and the interior mountains on the other provided a breathtaking view. They had a more relaxed life and enjoyed being in a new and safe city.

Something new was coming into their lives and they wanted to share the good news with his parents. They would soon become grandparents! Martina's pregnancy had made her more beautiful than ever they told her. She looked great and was healthy. They exchanged communications via Skype so that they could see her pregnancy as it progressed. They were utterly delighted.

As Martina's parents had both been murdered when she was only a child during a deadly firefight between two mafia gangs, Alfonzo parents would be the only grandparents.

She was less than two months away from delivering what her doctor fully confirmed to be twins, two very healthy boys. To the delight of the future grandparents, they were invited to come to visit as the date of delivery drew close. This had definitely brightened Alfonzo's life. They were more than eager to take on the long trip to be there as their grandchildren would arrive into the world. Martina and Alfonzo would be happy parents of two twin boys.

Real happiness had been a word of no real signification for such a long time for them. The good news had spiked what was for a long time a dimmed fading candle. They were so grateful to be able to feel real joy again. They would patiently wait for the right time to get on the plane.

Chapter 15

The unimaginable

Parenthood was not meant to be for Martina and Alfonzo. Despite her advanced pregnancy about to come to term, she was still doing some errands as always accompanied by one of her maids in case her babies would unpredictably signal that they were ready to come into the world. They shopped in the city nearby and that day, Martina was not prepared for what her destiny had in store for her.

Alfonzo was not with her, one very rare instance where he was on another errand, intending to surprise his wife, buying what seemed like a whole store to fill the baby's room with toys, and clothing, everything a mother would need to care for her babies. It was a very happy shopping spree for him and he couldn't wait to get home and lay out all the goodies he had purchased. He wanted to surprise her, bring her up to the room and turn on the light.

An ambulance was called as Martina had collapsed on the side walk, just about to enter a baby store. Alfonzo was contacted by his maid from the hospital. He rushed out from the store like he had never done ever before in his life, leaving everything he had purchased behind him.

In less than half an hour, he was at the hospital; he met the maid who told him everything that had happened. Martina had been immediately brought into surgery and the doctors told the maid that they would do everything in their power to save her and her babies. When he arrived, he saw policemen interrogating his maid and taking her testimony.

Alfonzo joined them and he went through the same type of questions but as she was so shaken by the news, they understood that it was not the right time to prolong the discussion.

She kept saying that she couldn't tell where the gun shots had come from. Actually, nobody heard any gun shots. It is just when she saw Martina collapsing on the sidewalk in front of the store that she realised that she had been injured. She was bleeding profusely and this is when she screamed for help and a passerby called an ambulance.

During all this time, Alfonzo realised that the ties he had wished to cut off forever were still there as strong as ever. Despite all the efforts they had made to separate themselves from Paolo and the mafia, they had been found. He had no doubt that this was the case. The surgery lasted six excruciating hours.

The main surgeon, a young Asiatic man finally came to him to give him the data about the surgery. Alfonzo immediately ran to him to find out the condition of his wife and babies.

- We are very sorry to say that we couldn't save the babies. A very saddened doctor told him. We did everything possible to revive them to no avail. Martina has been saved but I am very sorry to say that she will never be able to walk again. Her spine was severely injured by the bullets; her lower back nerves has been severed in such a way that nothing could be done.

The internal hemorrhaging throughout the placenta was so great that it cut off the oxygen to the babies. While we tried to revive them with an immediate caesarean operation, it was too late to do anything. She is now resting in the recovery room and you will be able to see her in about an hour or so. I am really, really sorry, he said, holding Alfonzo hands.

The doctor was very overwhelmed at having to give him the news. He kept saying that he was very sorry that he could not do any better; that he and his team of doctors and nurses had done everything to avoid the unavoidable. While the ambulance was fast in getting to Martina, the wounds were very damaging; there was nothing more that could have been done.

The doctor however could only stay for a few minutes as he had to attend to another patient who was ready for surgery.

The maid fell on her knees, uncontrollably crying.

The upset was so great that Alfonzo felt that his heart and head would explode. His heart was broken; he sat on one of the visitor's benches and cried as he had never cried before in his life.

They waited for the OK to see Martina in her room where she was recovering from the surgery.

As she opened her eyes, she saw Alfonzo sitting near her bed, his face in his hands and she could see that he was crying.

- Love, what has happened to me? She was barely able to whisper to him. Why are you crying? She asked while under the influence of her painkiller which made her feel numb all over her body. She had no idea how and why she had ended up in a hospital bed.

- Martina, Martina, Alfonzo came to her bed and tried as best as he could to take her in his arms. He kept crying. He didn't have any force left in him to tell her what had happened to her.

Alfonzo held her in his arms until two nurses came to the room to make a thorough check of the state of bandages and painkiller dosage.

It was a day later that Martina was told what had happened. She screamed in horror as she was told that she had lost her babies. She kept screaming No, this is not possible, No, this is not possible. Everything was spinning uncontrollably in her head. The medics had to administrate her drug to calm her down.

When she had gained enough strength, Martina and Alfonzo were told that they could see their dead infants at the hospital morgue. It was the most heartbreaking moment of their lives. Only six weeks away from coming to the world, there were two little bodies, one beside the other on a stainless steel table. This horrible picture of two little souls they never had the chance to hold in their arms and watch them grow had gravely hurt them.

***

Not long after they left the hospital, they had arranged for the funeral of their babies. Their grandparents would attend their burials instead of their happy home coming, watching the wheel chaired mother and the father placing two white roses over their tiny coffins saying goodbye was the saddest day in the lives of Alfonzo's parents. Their little bodies had been buried in the closest flower garden to their home, the rose garden, so that they could have her babies close to them and their hearts.

While there was nothing to yet identify them on their granite tomb stone, as both grieving parents wanted to take their time and chose something very meaningful for their little ones. They finally agreed on what to write and this is what they decided to get engraved on their tomb stone: "Two angels lie here. Sometimes we smile... We know you're near. You left with LOVE when you flew away, and a piece of us went with you that day. As the years roll by, we will not the same. But in our hearts you will remain."

Alfonzo now looked like a man who had aged 20 years during a very short period of time. It was so devastating for him.

It was very difficult to say, by looking at Martina and Alfonzo, if they would ever be able to fully recover from such grief and pain. Only time would tell.

No matter what the weather, Martina made it a habit to go see her little ones and attend to the flower garden daily.

While she couldn't leave her wheelchair to pull the weeds out or trim the various wild rose plants, she guided Alfonzo and her maids in order to make the place the most beautiful possible.

Chapter 16

The maid's secret

Out of the criminal investigation, there had been no findings that could significantly lead to identifying the criminal or criminals involved in this murder attempt. Nothing had helped the investigators no matter how many surveillance camera videos had been provided for that day. At the time, when Martina and her maid went shopping, it was during the afternoon and the main street of vendors and stores was very crowded.

All they could see was when Martina collapsed. There were several angles showing her when she got hit but they were not able to detect anyone around her targeting her with a gun.

Whoever had committed this horrendous act had probably used a silencer in order to not create panic within the crowd but to get close to her and be able to escape after the shooting.

Something had always remained in the back of his head. Alfonzo felt that there was a missing piece to the puzzle that had not been revealed.

He deeply felt that it had something to do with Paolo. He had no proof but he was so convinced that it had something to do with him that it was as if he was ready to lay his hand over a fire and be certain that it would never burn.

One day, as Martina was resting in her bedroom, Alfonzo approached his maid and invited her to come and sit outside on the patio with him.

- Imie, do you remember what the passerby who called for the ambulance looked like? He asked his maid.

- I don't know sir, I am sorry, I can't remember.

- Was it a man or a woman, he asked.

- It was a.... it was a man.

- Please try to remember, Imie, I need you to make every effort and try to remember what you saw.

She quickly became very upset; the grieving of the incident had definitely taken a toll on her. She started to cry and while apologizing, she genuinely made every effort to help him resolve the murder attempt on his wife.

- Can you draw his face, how he looked like, he asked.

He handed her a note pad and a pen.

Her hands were uncontrollably shaking but after a while, she was able to draw the sketch of a man's face. When Alfonzo looked at this, he sprang out of his chair.

- Why did you draw a darker line under his left eye?

- Because this is what I remember now. She had drawn what looked like a deep scar mark just under his left eye.

All the while, Martina had silently managed to position herself in the living room, just in front of the French doors opening onto the patio. She heard everything of Alfonzo's conversation with the maid.

She wheeled herself outside, joined Alfonzo and Imie and picked up the note pad in and looked in disgust at the drawing.

- My God, Alfonzo, what is there for us to do if this is really him?

The maid then confessed to them that as she was so terrified about the situation, that she had not told the investigators about him. She couldn't help it but thinking about this man that she had seen on the yacht so many times, that giving the investigators this data would put them more at risk and provoke a bigger situation than the present one.

She had probably saved their lives by not igniting a fire in the situation. They were appreciative that she had kept the secret to herself.

- I wished to die with my secret. I do not wish he harms you more! Cried Imie.

- Don't worry, Martina reassuring her, I understand what your intention was and I would have probably done the same. This was the right thing to do; now that we know, there is something that can be done about it.

With this new declaration, they realised they had to become more reclusive but at the same time more ready for what would be coming their way. They made it a custom to always carry their guns loaded and ready.

Chapter 17

More tragedy on its way

Later that same year, the stock market took a very deep plunge to a new low and the value of real estate shot down and Dream Investments old properties were no exception. Alfonzo had managed to miraculously sell it in time for billions to a very renowned Canadian trust fund firm who believed that it had a great potential for growing their value in the market.

His lawyers did a remarkable job and were abundantly rewarded. Their execution under his name was simply irreproachable on all angles. The course of actions was legitimately administered as everything in the Dream Investments had always remained under one owner, Alfonzo's. It was a clean and transparent transaction.

His lawyers had exerted their brilliant expertise in dealing with the buyers in the same way as an expert lapidary artist is able to cut and polish rough to the perfection of the final product.

There was after all no trace of Di Salvo's involvement in the business. Soon after, the financial markets took a drastic dive and while some of the investment companies raised back to previous and even higher levels of performance, Alfonzo's ex-company had never fully recovered since the sale. Furthermore, a leak in the media had surfaced where Alfonzo Pacchiano had predicted the fall of the market not long before the sale transaction and sold it on time in order to avert his company's downsize in value.

More offending than what had already been exposed were claims included in this same anonymous memo to the press, that he had ties to the Sicilian Mafia and that he had fled the country in order to not be exposed to upset investors asking for justice and retribution for their losses.

They would be soon discovered living in Southern Asia and their whole cover had now been completely exposed.

The goal was to obtain enough evidence to press charge and identify them as fugitives. The Canadian judicial authority could then immediately start the procedures to arrest them, push for extradition and return them to Canada in accordance with the laws.

The media headlines were striking: "Canada investigating Dream Investments ex-owner billionaire believed to be a runaway from justice". The whole article gave a very detailed track of Alfonzo Pacchiano's shady ties with the Sicilian mafia.

The article included his parent's past which had forced them to close down their pizzeria under uncorroborated reasons. It also included the suspicious death of a renowned ex-Swiss German banker while cruising on their yacht several years back that had not yet been resolved.

Someone had definitely opened the can of worms. While anonymous, these allegations could come from anyone who had been close to or associated with Dream Investments personnel, investors of any other individuals who had a vested interest in the company.

A great sense of paranoia kicked in at the news that they had been exposed. They'd been alerted by Alfonzo's parents as they watched the TV late news that day. Martina and Alfonzo decided that they would confront these allegations head on. They didn't have any other choice than to pack up and return to Montreal. They knew that their freedom was at stake if they were not to openly come in and defend themselves.

- What do I have to lose at this point! Said Martina. They fucked up our lives; they killed my babies, what else we have to lose Alfonzo, nothing! We have to return to Montreal and denounce everything that has happened to us. We do not have the choice. We are not going to jail for this!
They were willing to fight back while looking for a solution to denounce Paolo's operation, wanting to make a point that they had been the victims of the whole plot against them. They knew that this would only be the commencement of hostilities towards them. They had to strike back.

They got in touch with their lawyers to deal with this legal challenge. They knew very well they needed the best to tackle the situation and come out of it victorious. It would not be an easy way out but they were ready to do anything in memory of their sons.

They sadly handed pink sheets to their loyal chefs, maids and guards and closed down the place.

Before they departed the country, Alfonzo pushed Martina's wheelchair up to their rose garden for the last time to pay their final visit to their sons 'grave.

They made a solemn promise to them that they would soon come back victorious and clear of all the accusations against them; that their son's deaths would not be in vain.

Chapter 18

Dealing with the rules of law

La Prosperità Firm specialized mainly in international matters such as assistance in complex legal issues that required an understanding of political sensitivities and the need for a combination of strategic thinking and tactical excellence.

This is where they had made their reputation. They were brilliant lawyers who were not afraid to challenge the rules as they always found a convincing way to make any sceptical jury, witnesses or judges read between the lines with that which they persuasively illustrated in their favours.

The highly regarded lawyers were certainly not about to put their reputation in question. The charges were a major challenge to surmount but their brilliance had always guided them to victory and they didn't intend to see this case any differently than the others they had dealt with over the past 30 years.

They were the unrivalled champions of manipulation; they knew what words and expressions to use in a fully orchestrated fashion which would guide people through the emotional scale the way that the best actors on Earth would never be able to succeed in doing. Everything of course backed by their rules and the laws calculated interpretations used towards their defence arguments.

They had always managed to stir the pot and hit the bull's eye, surprising every one because their calculation as to when to hit was very much unpredictable. Prosecutors facing them always had a very difficult time, they were so brilliantly unpredictable.

These men knew exactly what they were doing. Their retainers were exorbitantly high but to whomever their client was, they were 99.9% guaranteed a victory. La Prosperità would never take on a case where they would even see the slightest indication of a loss.

The 0.01% always, but in very rare instances where the decisions went against them, they won in courts of appeal for a variety of reasons including improper procedure and in one case even asking the court to change its interpretation of the law and accomplishing this.

Upon their return to Canada, Alfonzo and Martina met with them. They knew that it would not take very long to see their official summons to court being issued.

Their lawyers had worked out the amount of bail which would release them from legal custody; they had formulated a brief which they would submit to explain to the judge why they should decide the case in their favour against their client's charge. The lawyers had examined, before the trial, all the facts and documents in what was called discovery in possession of the crown and were prepared for the trial.

They had studied all the written statements by the plaintiffs stating the wrongs allegedly committed by the defendants. They were the masters of counterclaims which they were ready to bring to light while the plaintiff's claims advanced by the prosecutors would not stand a chance of holding up during cross-examination.

What they were champions of was the use of the ultimate weapon to defeat any prosecutors, jury and judges, their exculpatory evidence which explained, without any doubt, their defendant's innocence. Mistrial, caused by fundamental error was not part of their language. They were the masters of great chosen statements and influences.

During their initial hearing, the court proceeding in which Martina and Alfonzo had learned their rights and the charges against them, they were to be held on a bail of 10M$ US and their release had been obtained by agreeing to guarantee their appearance on the day and time appointed for their trial.

Chapter 19

Montreal Superior Court

Order in the court! Order! Thank you Mr. Millburn for your deposition, the court will now adjourn until tomorrow, 10 am.

The judged tapped his gavel a few times. Everyone stood up and watched him exit. The court room emptied out quite quickly and Alfonzo Pinocchia accompanied by his lawyers immediately left the court. Several security guards were waiting for them outside.

Getting in their car, Alfonzo and Martina were more than eager to find out what his lawyers thought of the first day of their trial. They were actually more nervous than usual, a nervousness that they had not expressed to anyone for a very long time. Alfonzo readjusted his red rose on his lapel as it had twisted out of position, he then asked his lawyers:

- What do you think so far about his arguments? Do you think that it will do anything for the judge's decision?

- Not a chance Alfonzo, you know that. We've worked with this judge in the past and we know what appeals to him. Not a chance that he will come up with a guilty verdict. Don't forget also, we have the jury who will have to be accommodated as well. We have already started to gain very important contact information which we will be able to use to influence them as well. It is all planned and you should not worry about this.

- I am starving, said one of them, how about a great dinner at Salumi Vino?

- Sounds good, how about if we meet in about an hour time.
- Will do, Ciao!

Alfonzo's driver dropped the lawyers at their office, near the court building and carried on towards the condo.

- I will not be going to the restaurant Alfonzo, I am too tired. I hope you do not mind, said Martina.

- I understand love; do you want me to cook something for you?
- No, I'll get something simple. I am not that hungry. I'll go for a nap now.

He kissed her and helped her to her room.

Later in the evening, as he returned home, Alfonzo turned on the light; he felt that something was wrong. His wife didn't answer the door. This was very unusual. As he went down the hall calling for her, his attention was dragged towards the living room where he walked over a trace of fresh snow melting and darkening the carpet.

While Alfonzo and his wife were not cigarette smokers, he smelled the odour and realised that that was what had dragged his attention to the living room. In the light of the moon's rays coming through the window, he saw a swirling line of smoke coming from a man wearing a fedora while holding a cashmere Corneliani coat over his shoulders. He was standing in front of one of the windows in his living room smoking a cigarette.

- Who are you? Alfonzo immediately asked, taking his gun from his left side of his pants.

The man turned towards him and smiled at him.

- Alfonzo, my friend, how can you not recognize me? I can tell that the trial is getting on your nerves.

Alfonzo immediately turned on the light.

- How did you get in? He asked

- Don't ask. It is not important for you to know.

- Well, it is important Paolo! What the f...k are you doing here? Why are you here?

- Relax Alfonzo, you know why. We have things to settle together. I have not heard from you for more than two years. No payments have come, nothing! I know, I know, you sold the company but it doesn't matter. You still owe me!

Alfonzo became frantic, looking for his wife. Everything inside the condo was dark and deadly silent.

- Where is my wife? Where is Martina? I just talked to her a few minutes ago.

- She is not here, Alfonzo.

Alfonzo ran to him, took Paolo by the throat and screamed.

- Where is she? She can't move on her own, you know that. She is in a wheelchair! You piece of shit! Where is she?

- You'll get your wife back when I get my money, simple as that. Paolo told him as he dropped his cigarette on the carpet and grounded it in with his foot.

- What did you do to her? Where is she? My wife has nothing to do with you any longer. She has quit! Leave her alone! Where is Martina?

Alfonzo uncontrollably screamed at him until Paolo took him by the cuff and said:

- Pay back your dues and you'll see her again. You do not pay and you won't. I'll be generous with you; after all, you married my cousin. I am giving you one week.

He let go, pushing him resulting in Alfonzo's falling to the floor as he walked out the door. This is when Alfonzo discovered that he was not alone. Two heavily armed masked men exited the dining room and walked out the door with Paolo.

Looking for his cell in his suit pocket, Alfonzo called one of his lawyers and urged them to come to his place.

In his situation he couldn't appeal to the authorities to protect him because of his mafia's connection and the current trial that would easily be thrown overboard. He feared years in jail.

They had to figure out a way to find Martina without their help. Martina was due to be present in the witness box in a matter of days.

Chapter 20

The witness's cross-examinations

This was a major difficulty to overcome as they entered the courtroom that morning. Lanza, their lead lawyer, explained to the court that due to a health problem, Martina needed to be excused. He presented a doctor's note that due to her physical condition, she needed a few days of rest. As her absence was presented as a voluntary and necessary absence after the trial had begun, due to the fact of Alfonzo being present, it was accepted by the judge.

If she could not be found before her turn to be questioned, this situation might, however, be used in their favour, if they could succeed in exposing without a doubt, that someone didn't want her to reveal something, that her life was threatened once again because it would expose the attempted murder situation. This was to be done only as their last resort. They however hoped that they would never need to go there.

Alfonzo was to be the first of the two to be interrogated, so it gave them a short period of time to locate her. While it looked more than a little bizarre that Martina would not be sitting at the defendant's table for reasons known only to God, his lawyers told him to trust them as they planned to utterly make the courtroom shake with what they would reveal about her.

But before they could get the whole story blown out of the water, the prosecutors had a long line of witnesses to cross examine. They were ready for it. They didn't have any reservations about winning the case. It could become the crowning jewel of their careers.

The cross-examination would take days. The prosecutors had several dozen witnesses who had dealt with Dream Investments. Many of them had declared bankruptcy not long after the company had changed hands. They were all asked for the record that each one of them clearly identify the defendants.

Each testimony was backed up with sufficient direct evidence and facts that this merger had ruined their financial wealth.

Every single witness had filed for legal action and a lawsuit against Dream Investments instead of the new company owners, based on the fact that Alfonzo Pinocchia had failed to perform his legal duty of involving his investors in the merger transactions, taking action on his own which had harmed the plaintiffs.

The evidence provided by the prosecution's side was overwhelming; one after the other, every single witness had exhibited plenty of evidence, from their viewpoint, to lock Alfonzo and Martina up for life while they would replenish their coffers from Alfonzo's fortune. What however played in Alfonzo's favour was the fact that during the time he was the owner of Dream Investments, there had been no stock downfall in the market. It only happened after he sold the company that the dive had taken place.

This was brought to the attention of the jury and judge as every single person who sat at the witness bench got nailed with the same argument that Alfonzo was not at fault and that they were going after the wrong target, that he was in no circumstance responsible for the new administration's modus operandi as he no longer had any part in it or any control over the new company.

They had no proof that Alfonzo had purposely sold his company because he had "predicted the downfall of the market". Not a single witness for the prosecution could present evidence anywhere that Alfonzo had received inside information that the market was about to collapse and that he had sold out in order to get way from eventual troubles.

These arguments were being weighed in the balance. Alfonzo's lawyers hit the bull eye one witness at a time.

While all of this was taking place, Alfonzo had managed, on his lawyer's advice, to hire two private investigators to find the whereabouts of Paolo Di Salvo. It was imperative that Martina be found while he was sitting in court, keeping his "cool" under this stressful situation, listening to all these accusations of having ruined the lives of so many. He hoped that Martina would be located and safely returned to him.

Everything went as planned and as predicted by Alfonzo's lawyers until a witness, the last one for whom Alfonzo's lawyers were not ready. She was Angela Krämer, the widow of the retired Swiss banker who had died aboard the yacht who was now saying that she had never believed he had died of natural causes.

Alfonzo's lawyers couldn't cross examine the woman that day. The judge adjourned right after her testimony. It would only be the next day where they could go and assault her story with their counter punch which they intended to do swiftly in order to suffocate her story. But with this cross examination being delayed for twenty-four hours, it gave a tremendous advantage to the prosecution's side. Not once had she mentioned Paolo Di Salvo in her testimony.

She had been blatantly saying that the Dream Investments sole owner, Alfonzo Pacchiano was the murderer of her husband as he had gotten his hands on his entire fortune.

Her testimony sent shock waves throughout the media. This had become the most mediatised highly reported trial in the world.

The court reporters now had a gold mine to use to their advantage. Numerous conspiracy theories followed nonstop and lent a hand in keeping the trial alive and more fascinating than ever.

Chapter 21

The next day at the trial

Adelgiese Krämer was prepared to be cross-examined. This time, it would be the oldest of the defendant's lawyers who would take on the challenge; the most famous lawyer in the country about to launch ahead on attack on this woman whom, he judged, to be the biggest threat to their case. Silvestro Lanza was not about to give her a free ride.

His stern look made her feel uneasy right away as he approached her in the witness box.

He asked her several questions about her husband's involvement with Dream Investments, what had he given to the company, etc. She handed out additional information along with all the paper transactions which clearly identified the various types of bonds and other company shares which were transferred to Dream Investments without her knowledge. It made her very suspicious when she had discovered what her husband had done. She suspected that he had done the deals under duress and blackmail and that he got murdered when he refused to continue while on vacation aboard Alfonzo's yacht.

Alfonzo stared at her, couldn't believe what he had just heard. He became furious at what he had just heard. His lawyers told him to calm down. She would soon be nailed for this.

- Mrs Krämer, while I am sorry to have to meet you under these circumstances; how did you come up with the narrative of your husband being murdered on the yacht when this court case is about Alfonzo Pacchiano trial? This trial is related, if I well recall, to dealing with financial embezzlement and theft. You have just at this moment while still testifying under oath that you suspected Alfonzo Pacchiano as the murderer of your husband. Do you have any proof backing your statements? Where you aboard the yacht when your husband died? How did you come up with this insinuation that he got murdered? In fact, the police report says they ruled out any suspicious circumstances at the time of this death.

- Objection Your Honor! Raised the prosecutor. I object to this question, it is part of her testimony and should be considered as an additional charge against the defendant.

The judge banged his gavel a few times to regain order in the courtroom.

- While I understand what you are saying, I'd like to give the defendant's lawyer a chance to elaborate on this matter. Carry on Mr. Lanza.

- Mrs Krämer, in accordance with and in virtue of the trial purpose, isn't it peculiar that you had yesterday purposely put on the table the death of your husband in order to accuse Mr. Pacchiano of the death of your husband? I have not previously seen anything in your written deposition to the court regarding this matter.

- Your Honor, I am requesting that this part of her verbal testimony be withdrawn from the records as there is nothing that has been previously provided prior to the trial.

The reaction in the courtroom was swift. Banging his gavel, the judge decided to directly interrogate Mrs. Krämer.

- Why now, Mrs. Krämer? Why do you imply that Mr. Pinocchia had something to do with the death of your husband?

- Because I am certain of it.

- Your Honor, please allow me to carry on; I have a few more questions for Mrs. Krämer.

The judge nodded, indicating that he could go on, not convinced that she was worthy of being believed.

- Mrs Krämer, I have here in the record that your husband was a very influential banker in Zurich, is that true?

- Yes indeed he was.

- Was your husband suffering from any illness or taking any medical drugs that would have made him not responsible for his financial transactions with Dream Investments at the time they had taken place?

- Certainly not, my husband was a very bright individual and had not suffered anything of the sort.

- Then, Mrs Krämer, would you agree with me that your husband knew what he was doing while investing with Dream Investments?

- I agree, but...

- Very well, Mrs. Krämer, I'd like you, since being under oath, to tell me that you have an undeniable proof that this man, as he pointed Alfonzo, is the murderer of your husband.

- Objection! Objection, the prosecutor shouted in the courtroom.

- She is trying to destroy the reputation of my client, I have the right to know if she is worth believing or not.

- Can you prove to me what you have just advanced Mrs. Krämer? Where you on the yacht when your husband was found dead?

- No.... I can't.

- Your Honor, I direct the jury to disregard her statement about the circumstances of her husband's death and ask that it be withdrawn from her trial testimony. It is solely an attempt to confuse the purpose of trial.

- I am done with the cross-examination, Your Honor. I have no further questions.

The judge invited the prosecutor and Alfonzo's lawyers to his bench. They whispered to each other, making sure that no one could hear what was being exchanged and agreed that in order to not direct the trial to a mistrial that they had to agree that this matter didn't belong in this court case.

- Members of the jury, you are instructed to disregard Mrs Kramer's latest statement.

As the lawyer left his place, the judge adjourned the court for the day. The judge announced the court would recess until the following day.

- We will proceed tomorrow at 09:00 AM with the interrogation and cross examination of the defendants.

The top lawyer had come out of it victorious. He had strangled the witness's testimony with his strongly built arguments. She couldn't go against what he had voiced showing this to be irrelevant to the case. He was done with her.

Chapter 22

The locating of the kidnapper's whereabouts

After they exited the courtroom, Alfonzo and his lawyers found one of the two investigators Lanza had hired to help Alfonzo find Martina was waiting for them. He informed them that they were moving ahead in locating Martina's whereabouts and they needed to all rendezvous at the lawyer's office to be further briefed.

At the briefing, he informed them that Martina had been located in a nearby suburb of the city. Not very long after Alfonzo had left for his dinner with his lawyers, she was seen outside their condo, being assisted by Paolo Di Salvo himself into a wheelchair bus.

They checked and it did not belong to the city transportation network.

He proceeded to show them what they had been able to find thus far. Using an iPad, the investigator showed the surveillance camera footage they had captured. They had succeeded in reading the licence plate of the vehicle and been able to locate the owner's home very early the next day.

What was equally interesting is that Alfonzo recognized the young woman who was in the presence of Paolo and Martina. Imie, one of the maids who, a few months ago, had revealed that Paolo might be the probable perpetrator in the shooting of Martina, was there.

Alfonzo couldn't believe his eyes. Could she be an accessory to Martina's kidnapping? It was hard for him to believe that she could. Imie had been a very loyal employee for years and he had no reason to doubt her. Alfonzo, knowing her, felt that she had probably been dragged into the situation as she might know too much.

Both investigators met the bus owner later that day; his bus was parked in front of his home. He said that had been called for his service as a paraplegic woman needed to be transported. He said that he had left her with the two men at 17 des Huards on Nun's Island. The driver explained that during the transportation, the wheel chaired woman was seemingly very upset; swearing a lot; presumably in what he thought was Italian.

The other young woman who was with her was trying to comfort her as best as she could to no avail. The man with them had expressed several times his disagreement and tried also to calm her down, visibly embarrassed by her. The driver felt very nervous describing the man; he had a very deep scar line under his left eye. The man gave him chills all over.

While they were very efficient in locating them, they couldn't call assistance of the police in the intervention; it would be too hazardous as the scene would soon turn into an explosive bloody brawl; Paolo would certainly call for reinforcements and per the lawyers' advice, they had to make sure that nothing could lead in the direction of the Sicilian mafia boss. It would completely jeopardize their arguments of Alfonzo's innocence at the trial.

Since locating them, the investigators had managed to park their car on a nearby dead end street and had been able to keep close watch on everything. They were very well equipped, using night vision binoculars and a high definition surveillance camera. They were able to observe everything outside and even see into part of the house.

The owners of this mansion were an old couple who had taken ownership of the house just recently. They were Sicilians and close relatives of the Di Salvo family. Their background check had no indication that they were directly involved with any mafia activities but the sophisticated network didn't leave any room for possible conspiracy theories. They were just an ordinary couple who'd fallen in love with the island.

After exposing the situation, the investigator had always remained in constant communication with his partner. For now, everybody was inside the house and everything seemed calm.

He had to hurry back to Nun's Island. He didn't want to leave his partner alone, making him vulnerable if his cover should be exposed. Alfonzo was informed later on that day that they would get her out when they deemed it appropriate.

It was agreed that they be left to do what they were expert at doing while Alfonzo would show up the next day in the court. It was his turn to be examined and cross-examined.

During the night, back at his house, keeping his gun fully charged under his pillow, Alfonzo, his eyes wide open, kept thinking and had sudden back flashes of Martina's wounds, the burial of their sons, and the declaration of Imie's observations of Paolo. Lying on his bed, his heart kept racing. It would be a very long sleepless night.

Chapter 23

Alfonzo Pinocchia trial

The courtroom clerk approached Alfonzo Pinocchia who sat in the witness box, to administer the oath as it was now his turn to give his version of the facts. He felt as being between two worlds. One of trepidation about his wife's disappearance and one on the other side that was attempting to destroy him.

His lawyer had to coach him through his emotions. He finally understood that he had to testify before the court and pray for the best for his wife.

- Please raise your right hand. Do you swear to tell the truth, the whole truth and nothing but the truth?

- I solemnly, sincerely and truly declare and affirm that I will tell the truth, the whole truth and nothing but the truth so help me God.

- Mr. Muller, please proceed with the interrogation of Mr. Pinocchia, said the judge.

- Your Honor, there is no question in my mind that Mr. Pinocchia is guilty beyond any doubt that due to his criminal behaviour, his continuous lies to the investors and exploiting the vulnerability of his clients where, in some cases, he has covertly taken advantage of them more than once is beyond what anyone in this court can comprehend.

- As shown here, please see exhibit "A" the forgery of his client's signatures, of signed and endorsed checks made to his name for the total of half a billion of dollars. This is what we know so far. There is a great possibility that it is even more than this amount. We are not talking about pennies here, Your Honor, we are talking about life savings, grandkids scholarships, and mortgages that some of his clients used to participate into something that was too good to be true. The bait was made too appetizing to resist.

Your Honor, we are dealing here with someone who has no heart and had no honorable reason whatsoever to misuse the money that he was given in trust for investment by these innocent victims. He is a criminal.

- Mr. Millburn, I can acknowledge that your statement needs to be done but the interrogation has to begin. Please proceed.

- Thank you Your Honor. Mr. Pinocchia, when did you start your investments company?

- Fifteen years ago.

- How many people have invested in your company?

- I would say several hundreds.

- And what were the services you were offering to these clients?

- Great return on every penny they invested in my company. The majority of the investments I made on their behalf were off shore, in the Caribbean Islands, Bahamas and Mediterranean area, several American and European cities as well, all in real estate.

- Was there any reason why you choose to invest their money off-shore?

One of Alfonzo's attorney objected to the question, challenging it as detrimental to his client stipulating that he might be labelled as a tax evader.

- Objection rejected, said the judge, Mr. Pinocchia, please answer the question.

- It was the best way to make great return and avoid unfair taxes replied Alfonzo.

- Then can you explain to us why, while you had such great returns, that you have sold your company without publishing the information to your clients and investors before the sale agreement with McDonald Investments Corporation?

- My lawyers took care of the transaction on my behalf and the information had been published in a timely fashion. Nothing that was done is against the law.

- I understand but don't you think that it might have made these people think that you had let them down, ignoring them by doing so? Did you receive inside information that the market would soon collapse and that it was time for you to sell Dream Investments?

- I never heard nor received inside information from any one about this matter. It was a matter of life or death for my wife and me! I have no other way to justify what I did.

Rolling his eyes and then looking at the judge and jury, the prosecutor took on a mocking tone.

- What are insinuating now? You were under threat and this is why you sold your company? Should I remind you that you are under oath?

- I know I am under oath and yes my wife and I were threatened with our lives.

Then, within the courtroom, lots of people became agitated, speaking loudly with their disapproval about what Alfonzo had just stated. Then, soon following what he had just said, the courtroom doors opened, Martina moving by herself, pushing her way down the aisle.

Imie, her maid and the two investigators were seen, entering after her in the courtroom. She joined the lawyers at the defendants table. Imie was seen standing, not far from the investigators at the back of the courtroom.

Alfonzo left the witness bench and ran to her. Everyone could hear him shouting Martina, Martina, you are safe!

The judge didn't know what to think in the presence of such a dramatic event. The couple had, without a doubt, indicated as if they had a genuine fear that this moment would never happen. The judge had never witnessed such a situation in his courtroom ever before. Banging his gavel several times after watching what was occurring; he indicated that the court would have a short recess before carrying on with the proceedings in two hours; time for the defendants and prosecutors to take a much needed breather.

As they consulted each other regarding the incident that had just taken place, the prosecutors felt that it was a made up dramatic, theatrical scene which would add up to what Alfonzo had already mentioned during his interrogation. They had been told that Martina Di Salvo would be late that day but still make it in time for her turn to be interrogated.

They agreed to keep on the course they already taken. They didn't intend to deviate from anything they were doing but keep their focus on exposing both defendants as being guilty beyond any doubt so they could successfully convict them for their crimes.

On the defendant's side, Alfonzo's lawyers were very happy to see that Martina had been rescued. They had reassured Alfonzo that everything would work as they planned all along. They felt confident that they could win out, using their arguments and told him to leave everything to them and trust them as they were sure that they were going to succeed.

All he would have to do is to calmly, as feasible under the circumstances, answer all their questions, not adding anything, just straight answers. It would do its magic.

Martina, following the court recess, would put everyone in the picture regarding what had transpired in her kidnapping. Alfonzo couldn't wait to hear what she would have to say. He was certainly very grateful that the investigators had pulled this off. While she didn't look as having been under physical duress, while her scars were invisible, he felt her anguish, it was overwhelming!

Chapter 24

A flawless attorney's performance

Prosecutor Millburn stood up and walked up to the jury members as Alfonzo sat in the witness stand.

- Allow me to emphasize this very important point to you. As members of the jury, as jurors you are not to be swayed by sympathy; this latest incident, while easily inviting emotional feelings to play into your heads. What has, in appearance, illustrated a reunion of two people who looked as if they had not seen each other in years; they were seen sitting together at this same place, at this defendant's table just a few days ago. Please do not be fooled; please instead stay focused on the reality and the facts that we are placing before the court. We are dealing with a grave situation that has affected hundreds of people.

He then walked towards Alfonzo.

- Your Honor, please allow me to carry on my interrogation of Mr. Pacchiano.

- You may proceed, said the judge.

- Mr. Pacchiano, please remember that you are under oath. His eyes were scrutinizing Alfonzo and were very intimidating to him.

- Do you recognize these people here who trusted you with your business?

- Yes I do.

- Please speak into the microphone Mr. Pacchiano.

- Yes I do.

- I'd like to present Exhibit "B". But before, Mr. Pacchiano, do you recognize that this is your signature?

- This is the signature of the owner of Dream Investments who had applied under his clients names for mortgages, loans, etc. Do you agree that this is your signature?

- It is.

- Mr. Pacchiano, would you agree with me that you have purposely and covertly taken advantage of vulnerable people to fill your pockets? Do you recognize the other signatures that imply that your wife is also guilty of forgery on your behalf in order to get the funds you intended to take from them?

- My wife and I have been threatened and coerced into this situation as we needed more revenue. But I have never taken money from them. The money came from the returns which were way over the maximum bracket agreements between us. I had no obligation to tell them that I had higher returns than those they were entitled to receive. This is completely normal in any financial institution. There is no bank or financial institution that will tell you how much they gain as returns from their investments. The loans I have taken for them had great returns, I have given them more than they could have ever expected. All along, during my running of the company, I have never stolen anything from any one of these people. I know it, they know it. That things took a wrong turn after I sold my company doesn't make me the author who would suddenly provoke something in order to crash the market. I am appalled at hearing all of these unproven statements. I find them very ungrateful towards me when it should be to the contrary.

- While you imply that you were well intentioned towards your clients, the evidence is overwhelming! You have profited from their trust for loan applications. You have travelled overseas to make the purchases of real estate. How could your clients be happy at the time that you forged their signatures one day and then they drag you to court for a law suit as per their testimony, it is the opposite that has occurred. How do you explain that?

- Please rephrase the question, said the judge.

- Your Honor, I am just trying to ensure that the defendant realises where I am coming from. Mr. Pacchiano, do you understand that their lives have been ruined?

- I understand their upset but I am not the one who has created this financial market devastation. I see that you are insinuating that I have but I did not! There is no proof that I have purposely done anything that caused this market to take a dive. You are accusing me of something that I have not done! My clients should tell you that for every penny invested in the company, they always had great returns. I am infuriated by having heard from their mouths such accusations when they were always thankful to me to my face. I have never hidden anything from them. They agreed to cash their bonds, to sell some of their stocks and hand them to me. There was nothing wrong with that. This is the way financial investment companies work. Alfonzo had become very upset as he couldn't allow himself to sit there and be thrown into the lion's den without a fight.

- Do you plead guilty to any charges against you in this court?

- No, I am NOT guilty!

The prosecutor ran out of arguments. He had no proof of what he was advancing and while being very much aware of this fact, he had tried to pull a few strings with the defendant hoping that something would come out of the magic hat, something that nobody could have predicted to be revealed. His strategy had failed badly.
Standing in front of Alfonzo, the prosecutor looked at him and turned towards the judge.

- Your Honor. I have no further questions.

- We will now proceed with the defendant's lawyer for cross examination. Please proceed.

- Thank you Your Honor. Mr. Pacchiano, would you please tell me all about your company purpose?

- Dream Investments was a multibillion dollar company. I was the sole owner of the company and worked very hard to expand it and make into as a Canadian and internationally recognized icon. I am very proud of what I have achieved. My parents, young Sicilian immigrants, gave me the opportunity to grow up in this promising land and wanted the best for me. I am eternally recognizant for coming to this country.

- Were your client's right to trust you, Mr. Pacchiano?

- Yes they were.

- Why then would they come to this court and file a suit against you?

- This is one of life unjust situations; this is what I have to say about this suit. While this is very unfortunate as they have lost a tremendous amount of money, they are wrong in targeting me. Someone went to them; they were influenced and convinced to attack me instead of targeting the current company, which is not taking any responsibility for its failure and giving them explanations. I do not know their mode of operation; I do not know why their stocks fell. I have nothing to do with them and I am not guilty for their misfortunes.

- Do you feel that this is a complete conspiracy from these clients to gain access to your fortune to make up for their losses with the other company?

Muller immediately stood up, opposing this question.

- Objection Your Honor, I object about this question. It is implying that my clients are thieves which are quite the contrary.

- I want to know, replied the defendant lawyer, it is vital that we know. He is the one being targeted, not them!

- Objection rejected. Carry on Mr. Lanza

- Thank you Your Honor, Mr. Pacchiano, do you feel that this is a complete conspiracy put forward by your ex-clients to gain access to your fortune to make up for their losses with the other company?

- I do.

- Your Honor, I want to make it clear to the jury members and to everyone sitting in this courtroom that my client had not one single time overtly or covertly intended to harm his investors. The prosecutors have not found anything other than their client's testimonies which had done nothing to prove that he was the perpetrator of their misfortunes. This is an utter alteration of truth. Quite shocking!

Lanza had reached new heights as he could see the judge, the jury and crowd's reactions as he completed his arguments. He had definitely once more hit the bull eye.

- I am done with my questioning of the defendant for now, Your Honor; Lanza asserting his prodigious argumentum ad populum directed to the jury and passed by the prosecutor's table.
He could tell that the prosecutors were soon going to run out of arguments.

- Mr. Pinocchia, you may step down, said the judge. The court will now recess until tomorrow 09:00 AM for the interrogation and cross examination of the second defendant, Mrs Martina Di Salvo. He tapped his gavel a few times and left the courtroom.

While the defendant's lawyers were packing up their material, they felt very satisfied with their performance and congratulated Alfonzo for his courage in confronting the prosecutor the way he had flawlessly done.

They were glad that Martina had made it to the court safely. She certainly needed some time with her husband. Her forty eight hour misadventure had certainly taken a toll on both of them.
Round two would be as interesting as the first one, expressed Lanza while shaking hands with his partners.

From his lawyers' evaluation on the matter and what they had so far achieved, they asserted that it would only be a matter of a few days before the jury come up with a not-guilty verdict. The momentum was moving towards their side and they were confident that they would hands-down come out of it victorious.

Alfonzo, Martina and their lawyers were expecting to soon meet the two investigators along with Imie who would give them their accounts of how Martina had been rescued from Paolo. They exited the Palais de Justice Building and Imie along with the investigators were nowhere to be seen.

This had raised a few questions as to why they were not there as expected. While they didn't exchange anything verbally inside the courtroom, they expected them to be outside as it would be logical that they'd be there for them.

Their absence gave them very uneasy feeling as there was no indication from them that they would be leaving so promptly. They had remained at the back of the courtroom for the entire duration of Alfonzo's lawyer's questioning.

For security reasons, Alfonzo lawyers were very cautious about receiving instant messages or emails while inside the court. While their communication system was very up to date with the most sophisticated protection imaginable, they had always made it a rule that it was a no-no to receive anything while inside the courtroom. They always had taken this matter very seriously.

As they got into the car, while Alfonzo sat Martina inside of the car, one of the lawyers folded her wheelchair and put it inside the car trunk.

Alfonzo attempted to get hold of one of the investigators and he got a dead line...

While Alfonzo and Martina were confident that they would succeed in winning their case, they were not as sure as to where their fight for justice outside the courtroom would bring them.

The two investigators were not reachable; they had no clue as to Imie's fate. They felt that they were getting very close to a quicksand situation. People had disappeared before them without leaving any trace.

They intended to definitely leave the town for good, sell their condo and quickly return to Philippines and their private island.

Chapter 25

Loyal until her death

They were all sitting at Alfonzo kitchen table, sipping glasses of red wine while Martina told them what had happened 48 hrs ago.

As soon as Alfonzo left to meet his lawyer's friends at the restaurant, she heard a noise coming from the hall. She thought that it was probably Alfonzo coming back as he might have forgotten his wallet or something. She didn't pay any attention to it and soon fell asleep. Then, a man covered her mouth with a scarf and another pulled her in his arms and sat her in her wheelchair. She was covered with a blanket and taken out of the condo.

She soon realised that she was in the company of Paolo and another man she didn't know. She was placed inside a special bus for special needs transportation.

She tried to find out what was going on, what he wanted from her, she kept screaming at him that he had already hurt them enough; having lost their babies. Being paralyzed from her lower back to her feet, she couldn't bear any more suffering other than that which he had already heaped upon them. She implored him to leave them alone, that she would not say anything to the cops.

Paolo and the other man insisted that she shut up. After half an hour, from what she could remember, the driver turned in a very dark alley where she was dropped off with them. A light then turned on and she could see that she arrived in front of a huge mansion.

She had no way of knowing which street or even if she was still in Montreal. All she saw was a very stylishly designed number 17 on the left outside porch giving way to the main door.

Paolo and the other man soon disappeared in a car and left her in the company of an old couple. She was not even sure if they knew each other. While they spoke fluent Italian, they were not related to the Di Salvo family that she knew of. She saw Imie who told her that she had been taken by Paolo soon after she left the island. Paolo was very mad at her and she had undergone a lot of questioning as to our whereabouts, where did we go, etc. She swore to me that she had tried to do her best to not reveal anything.

Then, they all heard the door's ring tone.

They were not expecting anyone. Perhaps they were the investigators and Imie they thought.

Not taking any chance, Alfonzo went to his bedroom and took his gun with him. He was not about to open the door without it.
He arrived to the door and demanded using his intercom who was seeking access.

- It's us someone replied, your investigators. We have more information to give you.

Alfonzo pressed the button and let them enter.

They obviously looked as if they had been mentally showered with ice. The only thing he could see that was the saddened expression in their eyes.

- We've got to talk, one man said.

He invited them to come to the kitchen where everybody was eagerly waiting to hear what he had to say.

- What, what has happened? We were looking for you and Imie when we got out of the courtroom.

- Imie has been killed! We left the courtroom but Imie was not with us. We finally saw her being pulled into a black sedan and someone droving away with her.

We tried our best to follow but we lost her. The city is very much a construction site and with many detours, we lost track of them. We however, continued in the same area where we last saw the car when we heard a female cries coming from what we guessed as being the back alley behind the burned structure of what once had stood as the IL Sicilian restaurant.

As they left their vehicle to get closer and try to locate the woman's voice in distress, they saw Imie in the middle of an old parking lot. The place was completely deserted and as they walked along, they finally spotted her by chance as they saw that she exhaled air which had created vapor. This is how they located her. It was otherwise so dark and cold around. Imie was on her knees in a big pot hole full of water, begging someone not to kill her. She was hysterically trembling, her hands attached behind her back with a plastic tie. She had been spotted due to the fact that her dark coat made some contrast between the ice and snow on the ground.

- You told them that it was me didn't you?

- What are your talking about? She asked.

- You told them that I am the one who shot Martina, didn't you?

- No, I told them that you were the one who called for the ambulance, that's all I have said.

- Liar! You f...ng liar! The man's voice indicated that he had a very strong Italian accent.

- Please Paolo, Please believe me, how could I know whether you did it or not? I do not know! Please, do not kill me.

- Too late. You've done enough damage already. You should have shut your f...g mouth!

When they finally moved closer to her, realising that she was definitely in real danger, they ran as fast as they could to locate whoever was threatening her with death. This is when they heard three quick pops and saw her lying in a pool of blood.

When they finally got to Imie, they heard steps running away and heard a car door slam and saw a car speedily driving away from the scene.

There was nothing they could do. She had been shot three times in the head. She was gone. They left the area very quickly, making sure that there was nothing, not a trace of anything that would indicate that they had anything to do with the murder.

Everyone was devastated. Martina couldn't contain herself and screamed in horror towards the man she now, more than anything else, hated the most in her life.

- How could he do this, she said, Imie, my poor Imie. Why did they do this to you!

Alfonzo was speechless. The idea of how evil Paolo could be surpassed anything he had ever imagined possible.

Chapter 26

Martina's court appearance

The next day, it made the front page of the Journal de Montréal, several other newspapers and news websites. The cops who arrived at the crime scene didn't find anything to correctly identify the victim. However, they later realised that Imie was not a Canadian citizen; she had entered the country a few weeks ago.

They did their best to put the puzzle together and a few days later during a press conference, they mentioned that she had no close relatives living in the city or the country. They however strongly suspected human smuggling for prostitution as the reason behind the crime. She was of Philippine origin. Nobody had come forward to claim her body.

They called for the population help to give them any information about her. They didn't divulge anything additional about the case, despite the bombardment of questions from the press as they didn't want to compromise their investigation.

The same day as this explosive news, Martina made her way into the courtroom, wheeling herself to the defendant's table and waited to be called to the witness box.

Her lawyers had previously taken the time to ensure that she would follow Alfonzo's steps, not say too much, just keep her answers as short as possible so as not to invite suspicion as to what could be considered information being purposely left behind during her statements. She understood what was at stake and she felt confident of being able to make her way through the prosecutor's questioning. The courtroom was as crowded as ever. The court reporters were all eyes on her. She was impressively a very beautiful woman. Many had mixed opinions about her.

- Please raise your right hand. Do you swear to tell the truth, the whole truth and nothing but the truth?

- I solemnly, sincerely and truly declare and affirm that I will tell the truth, the whole truth and nothing but the truth so help me God.
- Please state your full name for the record.

- My name is Martina Di Salvo.

- Mr. Muller, please proceed in the interrogation of Mrs. Di Salvo, said the judge.

- Mrs Di Salvo, you are the business partner of Alfonzo Pacchiano, aren't you?

- I am.

- You are evidently a paraplegic. However, many of my clients who have previously dealt with you have specified that it has not always been the case.

- Objection Your Honor, this question has nothing to do with the purpose of the interrogation, Lanza shouted.

- Sustained! Said the judge, please rephrase your question Mr. Muller so that we understand your objective.

- Your Honor, I question the physical situation of Mrs Di Salvo since my clients had stated that she was not always in this condition. I'll rephrase my question. My question then is: "Under what circumstances did you become a paraplegic?"

- Objection Your Honor, my client doesn't have to once again go through the painful experience she has endured. The prosecutor's intention is to place her in a very distressing position, thus profiting from her vulnerability to pressure her.

- I understand you Honor but wouldn't it be interesting to know the circumstances of her new condition?
Lanza knew exactly where he was heading. His long years of experience had always served him very well. He had to stop him the best he could.

- Objection Your Honor! I'd like to remind the prosecutor that we are not here to discuss Mrs. Di Salvo's physical condition.

Then, the prosecutor, ignoring his plea, carried on questioning her.

- Have you been threatened or coerced into this operation to the point that you have been shot in the back because...

- Objection you Honor! This is not acceptable!

Muller disrespectfully ignored Lanza's objection and kept staring at Martina.

- Would you describe your condition as being the result of your involvement with the Sicilian mafia? Have you ever been involved with mafia activities?

Lanza then lost it; the prosecutor's questioning had become vicious and much deeper in scrutinising Martina than he had done towards Alfonzo as he viewed it. He walked to the judge's bench, made his request to speak to him and whispered to him that throughout his entire career that he had never seen a prosecutor acting in such way and that his intention was to clearly mischaracterize the defendant's testimony. Muller then joined them and they started to argue, gesticulating with their arms and heads.

The judge then reminded them to respect the code of conduct in his courtroom and that he would not tolerate their behaviour. He threatened them with throwing the whole case out the window by calling a mistrial.

They finally calmed down and the judge told Muller to carry on his interrogation while specifying that he was however not to ask her anything that had to do with her physical condition.

Lanza scored once more, confident that the proceedings would carry on without any further intervention of that sort. Lanza and his partners had realised that Muller had certainly been fed additional information as they had suspected at the beginning of the trial. Lanza understood that he had been fed new information that could change the direction of the trial in minutes and that; he didn't want to see happening.

The judge had become definitely irritated! It was just passed 11:00 that he overpoweringly banged his gavel several times.

- We'll take a break for lunch. He looked at his watch and said: Will carry on at 13:00.

A few other bangs were heard and he expressively left the courtroom visibly infuriated.

Lanza was relieved to see the judge's decision to take a break. It was welcome. He would take this precious time to go over very important points which he was predicting Muller would use to trap her. She had to avoid this at all costs.

Chapter 27

Behind closed doors

- Justice Mercier, I'd like to take a moment to discuss the recent turn of events with you.

Lanza appeared in the judge's chamber surprising him as he was answering a text message on his blackberry.

- What is it that you want Lanza? You know that you are taking a risk here; you know that you shouldn't come here.

- Well, I thought that it was necessary that I remind you that you have committed yourself as a judge to ensure the procedures do not get compromised. I have a strong feeling that Muller's intention is to force my client, Mrs Di Salvo to derail and go on a complete different path which would bring the case to halt.

- What do you mean, Roberto?

- Well, as you have observed and while I am very recognisant that you had decided to take a recess for lunch, which has given me the opportunity to discuss the situation with my client, Muller wants to derail my client. Don't you see it being a real threat? I think that he was given additional information following the submission of the filing of the suit.

- I got what you said but I will not further discuss this matter with you. Let's see what ammunition he brings during Mrs. Di Salvo cross-examination and I'll intervene as necessary. Do not worry, I'll use my power.

- Thank you Justice Mercier. It's always great to do business with you. Can't wait for summer, you owe me a round of golf, don't forget.

Lanza left the room smiling and joined his lawyers and the Pacchiano. They had a few minutes to ready themselves for another round of Muller's attacks.

Lanza felt confident after this private meeting that everything would follow suit the way he had intended it to and they would win the case.

Muller felt that he had something up his sleeve. Couldn't prove what he felt while looking at him but it was really odd to see Lanza looking so relaxed and at ease when he had witnessed seeing him standing furious before the judge a few hours ago.

- As you are ready, Martina, just a few things to go over. Do not extend your answers to give him fuel to burn on. Keep your answers short, nothing additional to say. He is a real master at pulling more strings than necessary. Remain careful and take your time before answering. You do this; he will soon run out of questions. I assure you.

Martina knew exactly what he meant. Muller's questions were as stabbing as a knife and she was not about to give him stones to sharpen it further.

Lanza, her lawyer felt that she had nerves made of steel to confront the situation head on. She had gone through a lot before in order to arrive at this day and plead not guilty. She told him that she felt strongly enough that she would be able to stand before anything that might happen in memory of her babies. She then was called to the bench.

Chapter 28

Strike Two

She rolled her way to the bench. All eyes were on her. Muller was ready and looked at the judge, waiting for the call.

- You may proceed for the interrogation Mr. Muller.

- Thank you Your Honor. Mrs Di Salvo, I want to remind you that you are still under oath and I'd like you to answer this question. As you see here, as he presented her samples of forged signatures which she had used for various loans and financial investments and cashing of bounds, you have purposely abused your clients. You have forged their signatures in order to enrich yourself. Did you or didn't you use your influence to make your clients agree with your actions?

- No, I haven't.

- Well, I am not convinced that this answer will do you justice. Please elaborate how you consider these actions not being criminal.

- I have done it with the best intentions. Many of my clients were getting on in age. They couldn't do what I was able to do. I did many errands for them at banks and financial institutions. They were all aware of my actions and were more than happy to see me when I returned and presented them with very fat cheques. I honestly do not understand why they have suddenly turned against me. It was all out in the open and done in good faith.

- So, you do not consider this as being a criminal act?

- No, I don't. If they had not been made aware that I was doing this for them, I can understand that it would be considered otherwise, but it is not the case. I swear they all knew what I was doing.

So far, so good, Lanza whispered to Alfonzo. He is hitting a brick wall.

- Do you recognize that this signature is of Mrs. Bernier's forged signature here?

- I do.

- Mrs Di Salvo, can you extrapolate further more on this, I'd like you to give me an example of what you have done for this plaintiff. I want to know if you can locate within this crowd one of the plaintiff and tell me how you have managed his or her finances while working for Dream Investments.

She moved herself to turn towards the crowd and looked to locate the best choice she could to make her point.

- I have located a person.

- All right, and who is this?

- It is Mrs. Bernier, this is she who is related to this exhibit you've just presented to me; she sits in the second row.

- Very well, Mrs Di Salvo, what have you done for her?

- Mrs. Bernier, a recent widow, had contacted Dream Investments saying that she had difficulties in understanding the investments her husband had done. She had discovered in his will that he had made several investments in several countries and that she had not the knowledge on how to deal with withdrawing the money. She figured out that with our help, she would be able to retrieve the money her husband had invested. I explained all the possibilities and how we could help her to also invest with us as she would get better returns. She agreed to everything, I did everything on her behalf and she was very satisfied that I had done it for her.

- Was she really happy that you have done this for her?

- Absolutely, without any doubt. She even gave me a gold brooch! Here, I'll show you. She looked for it in her purse and lifted it high in the air to prove that it was true.

The woman targeted sitting in the crowd felt as if she had become a melting ice cube as the jury and spectators looked intently at her.

- So, Mrs Di Salvo, you do not think that you've done anything wrong, don't you.

- I agree. It is sad that I have to sit here and have to defend myself from wrongdoing that I have never committed. I was dedicated and loyal to my clients. I cared for them and wanted them to get the best possible service. I have nothing to do with their financial downfall. The business has changed hands. I am sorry for what has happened to them but I am in no way responsible for their present situation. She had become very emotional at that point; she kept glancing at every single plaintiff sitting in the room. She shed a few tears which added drama to her ability to answer Muller's challenging questions. Muller knew exactly what effect she intended to create. He stared at her for a moment and then walked towards the jury bench; he felt that this was necessary as he saw each one of them displaying a negative expression towards the plaintiff Martina had brilliantly targeted.

- Again, I want to remind you that as members of the jury, as jurors you are not to be swayed by sympathy. This is exactly what she intends to do with you! Do not; do not be swayed by sympathy!

- Mr. Muller, do you have any more questions for Mrs. Di Salvo?

- I have exhausted the subject. I am done.

Muller sat back to his table, not knowing what to do. He had exhausted everything. She would not budge on anything he had asked her.

- Mr. Lanza, please proceed.

Lanza walked toward the jury as he wanted to make sure that the jury would understand that human emotion is part of the trial process.

- To you all the jurors, I want to remind you that nobody here is a robot. We have emotions and it is not wrong to feel emotions even though Mr. Muller has tried to convince you that it is otherwise. It is wrong! Mrs Di Salvo is an honest and irreproachable person who's always worked in the interest of her clients.

The judge banged his gavel, reminding Lanza that he had to cross-examine his client.

- Thank you Your Honor. Mrs. Di Salvo, can you please tell me how the agreement procedures were set up between you clients and Dream Investments?

- It is exactly as I said earlier. This was a person to person, very individual meeting with each one of my clients. I would carefully listen to their needs, if they wanted to invest with Dream Investments; I proposed to them the various options available. The process was not complicated, I just laid out what I would do, depending on the options they'd chose and executed what they wished for.

- Have you ever, since the sale of Dream Investments, contacted any of your ex-clients?

- No, I have not.

- Then, how did you find out what happened to them after the sale of Dream Investments?

- I only found out that their stocks and investments went wrong when I was handed an arrest warrant indicating that they had filed a suit against me and my husband.

- Please tell me Mrs. Di Salvo, did you ever covertly intend to steal money from your customers?

- No, I have never stolen money from my customers, overtly or covertly.

- Please tell me more about your way of making investments. I'd like you to brief everyone in this court room you way of operation.

- The money came from the returns which were way over the maximum bracket agreements between us. I had no obligation to tell them that I had higher returns than what they were entitled to receive. This is completely normal in any financial institution. There is no bank or financial institution that will tell you how much they gain in return for their investments. This is exactly how I have been operating.

- Do you plead guilty to any charges against you in this court?

- I am NOT guilty!

- Your Honor, I have nothing more to add at this point.

- Very well, I now invite the prosecutor to make his closing argument. Mr. Muller, please proceed.

- Thank you Your Honor. Muller took a deep breath and made his way before the jury members.

- Members of the jury, my concluding statements are that you have been provided with all the necessary proof to find Mrs Di Salvo and Mr. Pacchiano guilty of criminal embezzlement, thief and psychological abuse of well intentioned people. They have abused their vulnerability to enrich themselves. They sold Dream Investments and never told them anything. I am referring you to all the document exhibits which, even the defendant has positively confessed to be fraudulent in nature. What else do you have to see before deciding a guilty verdict towards them? I am confident that you will see through the fog of emotional influence they attempted to blind you with, that they are beyond any doubt severely guilty. When you get together to deliberate this case, please remember that a lot of these victims are now living in poverty, they couldn't do anything to withdraw their money before Dream Investments changed hands. Your Honor, I am done.

Muller then returned to the prosecutor table.

- Mr. Lanza, please come forward and make your final arguments.

- Thank you Your Honor, he moved quickly towards the jury, silently walked back and forth a few times, looking at each one of them. He then moved towards his two defendants.

- These days, you can go to court and accuse anyone of anything. I have learned this from a long career where you have to defend people who have never committed any wrongdoing but because of grave mistakes by others, they tend to find someone else to accuse because they never take any responsibility for their own actions. It is also very deplorable that lawyers involve themselves in such despicable actions taken by the plaintiffs by using dishonest, immoral, or illegal methods to line their pockets!

- I want to remind you that Mrs Di Salvo and Pacchiano are not guilty of anything. I am telling you this simply because it is the truth. Everything they had done, every action they had taken was to benefit their clients and they held the same procedures until they sold the company. Not one of their clients had lost money while dealing with Dream Investments. None of them! You were shown several documents about their increased investment returns.

- It is really appalling that these same plaintiffs didn't show up to sue the company that had taken over Dream Investments! Weird, isn't it! Of course, they couldn't go after McDonald Investments Corporation, they filed for Chapter 11 – they went belly up, they declared bankruptcy! But, have they informed their clients about it? Not at all! So, nowhere to go but after Dream Investments that, by the way, no longer exists as an enterprise on paper! It is gone! How far do I have to go to tell you how this trial is a travesty? A vicious travesty which is being used to cover up for what McDonald Investments Corporation, the real target in this case, has done to the plaintiffs.

- Remember, members of the jury, said Lanza, you have to take a really good look at what has been the hidden purpose behind this trial all along.

Lanza also pointed out the danger that a jury may chose to convict a defendant who has not broken the agreements with his clients. While they could be looked into as unusual actions taken to serve their clients, everything had taken place with their mutually agreement. Something they had to really consider in that case implying that if what they had done was wrong, then the plaintiffs were as guilty as they were; meaning that they were directly involved, they were direct accessories for having encouraged and participated in what they now accusing the plaintiffs of doing which ruined their lives; which is absolutely baseless.

- Dream Investments is not guilty! And one additional point I want to make. I am entitled, as the defendants' representative to have the jurors sequestered to prevent them from being influenced by negative publicity. They must be secluded from any outside contact so that they won't be influenced during deliberations. I do not intend to see a verdict against my clients on the basis that there is a lot of prejudicial coverage about them in the newspapers.

He then turned towards the judge.

- Your Honor, I believe that justice will prevail. My clients are not guilty. I am done with my final argument.

He then returned to his table, glancing at the jury.

- Very well! Said the judge. It is understandable that the jury will not have access of the outside while deliberating in this case. The court is recessed until tomorrow 13:00. I will make my statement to the jury members before they deliberate and reach their verdict.

The prosecutor's team had obviously dreadful long faces; they had tried their best to prosecute Alfonzo and Martina but abruptly realised that their clients were as crooked as the defendants. There was not much they could do at this point.

On the other side, at the defendants table, Lanza and his co-lawyers were all smiles. It had been a great day!

Chapter 29

The Judge's statements

The courtroom was as crowded as ever. The judge made his entry, his long black robe flowing behind him, reached his seat and seated himself.

- After all the evidence presented, both sides have given their closing arguments. I will now make my statement to the jury members.

- We have reached the next step in the trial when you the jury have to decide whether the defendants are guilty or not guilty.

- Ladies and gentlemen of the jury, I am now going to read to you the law that you must follow in deciding this case. To prove the crime charged against the defendants, the prosecution must have proven these charges to you. If each of you believes that the prosecution proved all of these accusations beyond a reasonable doubt, then you must find the defendants guilty. But if you believe the prosecution did not prove any one of these accusations beyond a reasonable doubt, then you must find the defendants not guilty.

- Proof beyond a reasonable doubt does not mean beyond all possible doubt. It means that you must consider all of the evidence and that you are very sure that the charges are based on facts.

- Remember, "Not guilty" is not the same thing as "Innocent." If you, the jurors are unanimous in your decision, this is the jury's verdict. You have heard several witnesses testify, including the defendants. It is up to each of you to decide if you believe that these witnesses were telling the truth or not. You should consider how the witnesses behaved on the stand and use your own common sense in deciding whether or not a witness was telling the truth.

- Remember that it is up to the prosecution to prove the defendants are guilty. The defense does not have to prove the defendants are innocent; if the prosecution has not proven its case, then the defendants are not guilty. Also, remember that you can only say the defendants are guilty if the prosecution has proven all of the charges beyond a reasonable doubt. As I told you, beyond a reasonable doubt means that you must be very sure. That means that you will still be sure tomorrow or next week or next year. It does not mean any doubt you can think up in your imagination.

Judge Mercier explained furthermore the laws and rules that the jury must follow in deciding the issues of the case. He specifically underlined the importance that they had to decide on the facts and solely on the facts.

His speech lasted close to two hours and the jury was then dismissed to deliberate until they arrived unanimously at a verdict. They all retired to the jury room to begin their deliberations. Everything was to be, of course deliberated in secret.

Lanza was confident that it would just be a matter of a few days before he would see the jury foreman back in the courtroom and unanimously present a not guilty verdict.

Days went by with no word of the jury's decision. The deliberations were ongoing nonstop. Several times the judge was asked for answers to several of their questions related to the law.

From Lanza's intuition, he estimated that they could have some debates in regards to the voting of their verdict on each crime the defendants were accused of based on their examination of all the evidence provided.

It was far from being a light case of shoplifting. It was far more serious than that.

They had to agree on every point, discussing each crime the defendants were accused of based on their examination of all the evidence provided.

Chapter 30

The return of the villain

While waiting for the jury's verdict on their court case, Alfonzo and Martina had their premises under constant surveillance, having hired a group of ex-military personnel to assure their protection.

Despite the fact that they had good reasons to request protection from the cops, they couldn't take that chance. They had no choice at this point but to hire people who had security experience and worked privately. They were getting close being able to free themselves from these accusations and go back home. It was something that they were eagerly looking forward to.

Alfonzo did most of the errands as he preferred Martina to stay home due to her handicap that would make her vulnerable if another attempted attack should take place, he was always accompanied by unidentified persons who looked as ordinary as possible. They were however heavily armed and at the ready should anything suspicious develop.

He dined on a few occasions with his lawyers and discussed further about what he intended to do to bring down Paolo Di Salvo for the murder of their maid Imie and the kidnapping of his wife.

Martina and Imie were rescued from the old people's mansion by chance. Soon after they disabled the security system, the investigators had done a great job as they threw smoke bombs and flash bags which had overwhelmed everyone inside. This is when they grabbed Martina and Imie and fled the scene.

Martina and Imie feared for their lives, seeing these impressive men wearing gasmasks taking them and forcing their way out.
They were long gone before the ambulances, firefighters and cops arrived at the house.

Nobody inside could say anything as it would expose Paolo's plot; they couldn't discuss anything with anyone about the kidnapping of two people in this house. They were immediately warned of the bad consequences that would follow any revelations. The old couple pled innocence and underlined the fact that they had witnessed similar activities related to biker gang's waging war over drug trafficking in the area and that they might have been, like several of their neighbours, wrong targeted.

This was taken well as it was in fact an area where several gang related fights and brawls had recently occurred. The cops were aware of these activities and they were all under investigation. So, this would be an additional case within the lot.

As there was no further concern about their health, they returned to their house after undergoing a doctor's examination at a nearby hospital.

Alfonzo had to figure out a way to indict Paolo for his crimes while protecting his interest. He had to ensure that nothing would suggest that he was involved in any of Paolo's criminal activities.

This very topic would be a tremendous challenge but he was certain that something or someone would come up with help in providing sufficient evidence to put him on trial as a result. He wanted to finish him off one way or the other.

Chapter 31

Behind the scene

While Martina and Alfonzo were battling over their case in court, something was still brewing behind the scenes. Paolo Da Silva had gotten hit with a costly blow since McDonald's had declared bankruptcy; it had created havoc within his empire. The funnelling of their dirty money had come to an abrupt stop.

They had been introduced to the company that bought Dream Investments only on paper by Alfonzo's lawyers along with information on all the other investors. They were just, as many overseas investors dealing with Dream Investments. They wished to operate under a pseudonym and would only deal with them by financial wire exchanges.

Since this was not an unusual proposition on how they wished to operate, as there were many investors who wished to operate in the shadows for their protection, this had been all mutually agreed upon. The new owners couldn't tell any difference between them and the other investors. McDonald Investment Corporation had never suspected anything, they just appreciated the money they, along with the other investors, brought to their financial activities creating great profits.

But now, the whole thing was cut off. He had lost a tremendous amount of money since their bankruptcy and several billions of American dollars, that he had hoped to be successfully bleached clean from their underground activities, had been piling up in several bank accounts. He had nowhere to turn. There was a major danger that he would soon invite suspicions of undeclared earnings and questions regarding the source of his incomparable wealth.

He soon came under surveillance by several revenue agencies. While Paolo Di Salvo was not aware of the fact that these agencies were discreetly and quietly hunting him down, he however knew that he had to figure out something rapidly to avoid being caught.

Unless he could hook up with another investment company, start everything anew, he knew that he would be in a very dangerous situation.

The only thing at the time was that globalisation propaganda being pushed in every way possible by international bankers could play a major role and could heavily influence his future.

The intention behind the scenes was to convince governments and several other worldwide influential entities including the U.N. that it was part of the globalisation, that it was mandatory that all banking systems parallel their activities towards the same goal.

Paolo Di Silva had to find the connection that fit with what he would judge as being influential enough to get his money to start cascading again throughout several investment market vehicles.

Chapter 32

The Jury's verdict

The day they had been waiting for finally arrived. The jury had contacted the judge as they had unanimously come to their decision regarding the verdict.

The courtroom was filled to capacity. The court reporters were at the ready to type every single word and create a master piece of this historical and unprecedented verdict they hoped would go the way they wanted.

Everyone in the courtroom, the plaintiffs and the defendants were eagerly awaiting the judge to make his appearance at the top of the platform to read and hear what the jury had decided.

At defense table, Lanza along with his co-lawyers illustrated self-confidence while waiting for the verdict. He was calm as usual. Then the judge appeared and proceeded.

- We have now come to the day where we will know the fate of Mr. Alfonzo Pacchiano and Mrs. Martina Da Salvo and end this trial. Will the jury foreperson please stand? And would the defendants please stand?

Martina and Alfonzo holding their hands stood and looked at the juror.

- Has the jury reached a unanimous verdict? Asked the judge.

A man stood up and answered positively to the Judge.

- Yes Your Honor, we have unanimously come to a verdict. I'd like to hand you our final written statement.

The court clerk hurriedly walked towards the jury spokesperson who handed him the written verdict to give to the judge.

Judge Mercier silently read their statement and then handed it back to the clerk for the reading of the verdict. No one could tell what he had read. There was nothing on his face to indicate positively what the verdict could have been.

Each charge was read loud and clear:

- On the charge of theft, has the jury reached a verdict?

- We the jurors find Mr. Alfonzo Pacchiano and Mrs Martina Di Salvo not guilty.

- On the charge of fraud, has the jury reached a verdict?

- We the jurors find Mr. Alfonzo Pacchiano and Mrs Martina Di Salvo not guilty.

- On the charge of forgery and uttering forged documents, has the jury reached a verdict?

- We the jurors find Mr. Alfonzo Pacchiano and Mrs Martina Di Salvo not guilty.

- On the charge of false pretense, has the jury reached a verdict?

- We the jurors find Mr. Alfonzo Pacchiano and Mrs Martina Di Salvo not guilty.

- On the charge of identity thief, has the jury reached a verdict?

- We the jurors find Mr. Alfonzo Pacchiano and Mrs Martina Di Salvo not guilty.

- On the charge of laundering the proceeds of crime, has the jury reached a verdict?

- We the jurors find Mr. Alfonzo Pacchiano and Mrs Martina Di Salvo not guilty.

- Your Honor, we found Mr. Alfonzo Pacchiano and Mrs. Martina Di Salvo not guilty for the following reasons.

- First: Within all the evidence and documentation submitted to the jury members have we not found anything related to their activities which was unknown to the plaintiffs. They had all agreed that Mr. Pacchiano and Mrs. Di Salvo manage their money exactly as they were told would happen. There was nothing hidden from them. That they had taken actions which were not strictly per the law; we have seriously considered this situation the possibility that the plaintiffs are definite accessories to these unusual and unlawful actions. Therefore, they cannot with clean conscience accuse them now of something they encouraged them to do for them! It is simply incorrect and cheating!

- Secondly and most importantly, the loss of the plaintiffs' fortune did not fall under Mrs Pacchiano and Mrs. Di Salvo's management of their money. They lost their money while it was under the control of McDonald Investment Corporation. Dream Investments ceased to exist the day McDonalds purchased the company.

- The jury members had unanimously agreed that under these circumstances, events and mutual agreement within the plaintiffs and the defendants, that Mr. Alfonzo Pacchiano and Mrs. Martina Di Salvo are not guilty of these charges. It would also be a waste of time and money to continue the case in the court system. We have not found any proof of Mr. Pacchiano and Mrs. Di Salvo's had committed any negative influence on McDonald Investment Corporation. They had been long gone, close to a year before McDonald investments took a dive in the financial market and declared bankruptcy. For these reasons, I along with the other jury members have found Mr. Alfonzo Pacchiano and Mrs Martina Di Salvo not guilty of any of these charges and respectfully request Your Honor that our decision be sustained and approved.

- Order in the court! Order! Please, Order! The judge had to intervene as several opinionated and vulgar statements quickly followed the jury verdict.

- The jury is thanked for...Order in the court! Order!!!! The judge was about to lose it, slamming his gavel several times. Order! The jury is thanked for their work. You are now discharged and are permitted to leave the court complex. This acquittal formally certifies that the accused are freed from the charges on all of the offense, as far as the criminal law is concerned. The court accepts the verdict of the jury. Mrs Di Salvo and Mr. Pacchiano you are free to leave the courtroom. The case is now closed!

The judge left his bench and swiftly entered in his judge's chamber. The case was over and he felt very satisfied at the outcome.

The prosecution team had expected that some of the charges would stick, however very disappointed with the verdict, they felt they had done their best but their discontent could be read all over their faces. The next day the headlines in the media read as followed:

"An historic trial verdict in Montreal city!
The ex-Dream Investments owners who had sold their company to McDonald Investments Corporation - Alfonzo Pacchiano and Martina Di Salvo were found not guilty on all of the charges laid against them. The prosecutors will not, in this case, appeal. There are however a lot of unanswered questions as far as the Dream Investments activities, we will probably never find out the full extent of their activities. The court has reached new heights of justice since the plaintiffs in this case would have been as guilty as they had committed or agreed to commit the same crimes for which the defendants were being accused." said the juror representative this morning before Judge Mercier. This long and stressful trial of the defendants which seemed to have all the evidence necessary to successfully prosecute this iconic public figure is over."

Chapter 33

The trial's closing moments

After seeing the reasoning behind the jury's verdict read in the courtroom, all of the defendants' team along with Alfonzo and Martina were relieved with reference to the outcome.

They could finally close this chapter of their lives.

They rapidly left the court house and drove away to Alfonzo's condo in order to take a breather and celebrate.

There were things left to address which Alfonzo and Martina intended to confront head on. They wanted to take revenge for the deaths of their sons and of Imie, their maid. They felt that they owed it to them. Paolo Di Salvo couldn't get away with murder. He might have done it many times before, but this time, they didn't intend that it would be an option for him. They also wanted to arrange for a proper burial for Imie.

They anticipated leaving Montreal for good and as soon as possible and return to their island to start anew, to return to some extent to what could be described as a normal life.

Lanza laid several options on the table. However, confident that they could do something effective about it, Lanza requested that they would study the matter to find a way where they would be able to extradite him from wherever he would be situated to face justice. He was not a Canadian or even permanent resident. His only ties with the country were with Dream Investments. They had to figure out how to obtain strong evidences of Paolo's underground activities. This was the only option they judged at the time as being a sure way to get him.

They had to be more than careful as bringing this matter into view could affect the couple because of their direct past liaison with him. Paolo Di Salvo had to be prosecuted in a way so as not to expose Alfonzo and Martina's associations. It was a delicate two edged sword and very risky.

Lanza confidently stated to them that there was a way to nail him in to a corner where he would not be able to make or attempt to make any move to get out. He insisted that it had now become a personal affair and he wanted to deal with it personally. He knew everything about Alfonzo and Martina's downfall due to their association with the devil and while they had confessed their own guilt towards their wrongdoing, it was too outweighed by the hell that Paolo had put them through. It has become very personal for him to deploy all of what he knew to the attack and do whatever it would take to get Paolo squarely and violently separated from his freedom.

As Martina and Alfonzo couldn't directly get involved in the process, Lanza suggested to them that it would be better for them to leave Montreal and go home. There was nothing they could do. He would certainly keep them abreast of his activities and would pay them a visit once in a while to keep them personally informed on the developments. It would certainly not be a fast paced investigation; there was a lot of work to do such as finding his whereabouts, documenting his underground activities, locate where he has been stashing his money since he no longer had Dream Investments as a cover for his dirty money, etc. The task was immense but Lanza would make the proper contacts in order to build a team of private investigators and detectives, that he felt confident would be able to do the job.

Soon after, all their assets and bank accounts had been freed from the seizure orders the prosecutors had filed for their trial. There was nothing stopping them from leaving.

Alfonzo contacted his parents who were more than delighted with the news. He told them that he would soon return to the Philippines and would book a flight for them to come and visit. He couldn't wait to share his journey with them.

Martina contacted a real estate agent to take care of their condo sale. They then packed up and booked their flight to Hong Kong.

Chapter 34

Returning Home

Martina and Alfonzo took a last look at Montreal as they flew over the city very early that morning on their way to Toronto. Sour feelings of their last ordeal added to their already painful past association with this city.

They landed in Toronto an hour later.

As they were sitting in the VIP lounge waiting for their call to board their flight, Alfonzo made a call to his parents.

He felt like a kid who was finally able to confess that he had been wrong to have put his hand in the cookie jar when he was not supposed to do so. He felt that he owed his parents an apology; he hoped they would forgive him.

Alfonzo recalled all his great moments at the IL Sicilian where he dreamed as a kid to become someone of whom his father would be proud. He had heavy remorse on his conscience towards what they had gone through because of his unethical choices in his life.

Their conversation was very emotional. Martina felt that he had gone through, like her, a severe emotional meltdown. Only time would be the healer in surmounting what had been accumulating for the last dreadful years.

Then, an Air Canada agent called for the first class and people with disabilities to board. Alfonzo said his goodbyes and hung up. He pushed Martina's wheelchair and they boarded the plane. The trip would also be very tiring as they would finally touchdown fifteen hours later.

All the way during their travel, they didn't exchange much in the way of a conversation; they didn't feel that they could freely communicate. They didn't have their security guards with them. They were on their own. It would only be upon arrival that Alfonzo would contact a private security agency to hire new security personnel.

***

They were finally awakened by a flight attendant; who informed them of their arrival.

They retrieved their luggage and exited the international arrival's gate and made their way to customs. Everything cleared and they called for a taxi to take them to the ferry and home.

 Accompanied by a luggage clerk, they waited outside for a taxi when they saw two men coming in their direction. They didn't know who they were.

- Mr. Pacchiano and Mrs Di Salvo, you are in need of protection. Paolo Di Salvo knows you are here.

- Who are you? Alfonzo asked.

The two men showed them their IDs simultaneously; they were from Interpol. They explained that they had been trailing Di Salvo for quite a while and that from wire taps and the intelligence information gathered so far, it indicated that serious attention had to be directed towards Di Salvo since he intended to eliminate both of them.

The two agents invited them to enter into their armoured SUV and leave the airport area. All the way during their ferry ride, the agents explained that Di Salvo had been under surveillance for several months as they had received several reports from different agencies worldwide that he was acting or to conceal or disguise his identity in order to legally obtain proceeds which first appeared to be originating from legitimate sources when they were not.

As the surveillance had increased and while gathering intelligence, a lot of suspicions were aroused which led them to conclude that this man was a serious criminal. His financial influence reached every corner of the planet and he was operating not only a wide range of financial crimes, but also benefiting from drugs, prostitution and suspected murders for which he could easily be jailed for the rest of his life. Illegally obtained funds were currently laundered and transferred around the globe using and abusing casino companies, intermediaries and money transmitters. In this way, the illegal funds remained hidden and integrated into legal business and thus into the legal economy.

While they were not cops themselves and couldn't by any means arrest him, their purpose was to gain the cooperation of local authorities, presenting them with all the evidences of his crimes for them to then successfully take him into custody.

They insisted that they would not press charges against them and assured them that they would be given immunity if they were willing to testify before a court as witnesses if it would turn out to be necessary to once and for all bring Paolo Di Salvo to justice.

As they discussed the mafia boss further , Martina and Alfonzo were told that two very important witnesses, they would not divulge them their identities, had been providing information to Interpol about Paolo Di Salvo about this matter along with this his direct involvement in Imie's murder.

While they had not communicated again with the investigators following their revelation that Imie had been murdered, they were however sure it was them. At the thought that they would make this move even though it could jeopardise their cover when they had addressed Imie's kidnapping outside the courthouse, they had never expected them to do this.

Per the agent's description, there was no doubt in their mind, it was definitely them.

The agents went on saying that they had been given immunity in exchange for their crucial information which they had given.

The Interpol agents certainly knew that Alfonzo and Martina were involved with the mafia affairs but they were the lesser of the two evils. They hadn't committed murder as Paolo had done.

They got onto the ferry which would bring them to Ariara Island. They were more than eager to return to the place where they had lived in happier times.

As they approached, they could see that tall grass overgrown everything around including their beloved rose garden.

Not expecting this at all, they saw Martina and Alfonzo move through tall grass away from the house.

- We will be back...said Alfonzo.

But he couldn't move the wheelchair forward any further; the density of the grass impeded it. He lifted Martina in his arms and carried on walking until he reached the area of the tomb stones. It was all covered with grass and the roses looked as if they had been strangled. It had become a very desolate place. The garden had been left on its own for months.

As they got closer to where they remembered was the area where their son's tomb stones were situated, Martina screamed of horror, the stones had been hammered down.

Hearing her screams, the two agents went to what they thought would be their rescue only to see a very poignant situation. Alfonzo was holding his wife while on his knees. They both were crying. Seeing the scene unfold, the agents stood there in silence and waited until they decided to leave the area.

They didn't have to wonder who could have carried out this repugnant act. It had to be Paolo Di Salvo, only this monster could be suspected as being the author of this despicable scene.

- We will get new ones, Martina. Our sons will have a new tomb stone and this place will never again be abandoned, I swear to you.

Chapter 35

Security Check

When they decided to leave the garden, the agents suspecting that the scene inside their home could have possibly gone through the same type destructive ordeal insisted that they inspect the inside of the house while Alfonzo and Martina keep their distance and wait inside the SUV.

Guns drawn, they went through every single room and didn't find anything that had been disturbed. However, while keeping silence and moving outside to the veranda, one of them indicated to the other that something looked fishy as they spotted a few surveillance cameras that seemed to be focusing on them. They couldn't tell if the reason behind this was because of motion sensors that would cause them to move or if there was someone remotely guiding them to focus on them.

They left the house and asked Alfonzo and Martina if they had installed surveillance cameras outside over their front and back verandas, and if this was the case, when and where they got them installed and to name the company they had dealt with for the installation of the system.

The questions gave both of them chills throughout their bodies; they had never installed surveillance cameras inside or outside their house they hadn't thought it necessary since they had security guards employed full time.

Upon further inspection, both agents realised that all the cameras spread outside hanging from the ceilings of both verandas were powered by a solar panel sitting on the roof. However, there was no connection wired to guide the viewing source. Everything was wireless and Wi-Fi.

They inspected inside the house to check if there were any types of routers and they found nothing.

The whole system could be run and accessed using a simple tablet or a smart phone.

Denying that this security system belonged to them, it became clear that further inspection of the house was necessary. They had to find out where the camera's transmission viewing was destined for. Until everything was cleared, there was no way for Alfonzo and Martina to settle back into their home. A necessary and exhaustive security inspection had to be done. There could be booby traps inside or outside just waiting for a proper signal and identification of Alfonzo or Martina to blow the whole place. It was essential for them to locate the source of the camera reception and uncover who was secretly observing the area.

Getting back to the SUV, one of the agents called for an elite team of IT engineers and bomb squad assistance to get this done within the next 24 hrs. They would be rushed to the island coming from several neighboring countries to give them a hand. They had to sort this out fast. The bomb squad quickly located explosive charges under both verandas and others placed inside with enough power to fully destroy the house.

It was good that Alfonzo and Martina hadn't moved closer to the house, they could only imagine what would have happened to them if they had walked up onto one of the verandas.

They immediately took the next ferry leaving the island on their way to Hong Kong and would stay in a hotel to which several security agents had been dispatched before their arrival. They were shocked to see one of the agents opening a briefcase and handing them false IDs, false credit cards, new cell phones and passports. Everything had been surprisingly set up for them way before their encounter at the airport.

The gravity of the event was overwhelming to Alfonzo and Martina. Their nightmare was obviously far from being over.

The agents drove them to Hong Kong where Alfonzo recognized the street heading to Pacific Place on Queensway. He knew that they were heading to The Upper House, one of the most luxurious hotels in Hong Kong.

A suite was already rented for them which included all dining services in their room. They were obviously not to be allowed to roam on their own throughout the hotel.

They couldn't tell how long they might have to occupy the suite. Nobody could guarantee that they would even be able to resettle into their house. Until the security inspection would be fully completed and all explosives located and removed, nobody could guarantee anything.

It was equally vital, for their safety that they did not get in touch with any relatives; the cellular phones they had handed to them were to be solely used to communicate with their security team. Their phone conversations would be connected to orbiting satellites instead of terrestrial cell towers. As they would tune them to communicate with them, a secret code would alternate every time they used a phone. It would instantly prevent any attempts of eavesdropping or breaking the encryption outside their network.

Chapter 36

The Mafia Boss

Paolo Di Salvo was brilliantly playing with the authorities in view of the fact that he had progressively developed this paranoia since Dream Investments had changed hands. When McDonald Investments took over Dream Investments, they made a complete change of the executive structure, placing their own personal in all senior positions. Unfortunately for Paolo, this took out his men who he had placed in the executive team of Dream Investments, leaving him with no control or inside information regarding what the company was doing.

He had since been warned, several times over the period of a year, that he was under surveillance. However benefiting from several professional technologists from all level of needed expertises, he succeeded in strategizing a game where his activities might be spotted inside a financial maze only to then disappear, this short trace vanishing at a blink of an eye.

He had connections around the world and people were either voluntary or forcibly made responsive to cover up for him. It had become very rewarding and lucrative as a side activity amongst government representatives and various banks owners.

Paolo Di Salvo has always been ready to pay anything to anyone who endorsed his activity. He had generously paid those who assisted him in locating new means of carrying on and covertly funnelling his money making it usable for him. He didn't care where the person was coming from. As long as they would meet his basic requirements after several screenings for their genuinity, it had greatly enabled him to stay out of the hands of the law for quite a while.

His financial operations ongoing, he remained at his summer villa in Marsala. Its isolation in itself gave him the necessary cover he needed.

Eliminating Alfonzo and Martina was still something on his mind. He had to viciously address this as he suspected them of being the ones behind his ever-increasing problems. He found them to have cost him a lot and as long as they remained alive, his empire continued to pour a lot of money into getting rid of them and would remain to do so until the day they would be eliminated.

Upon requesting his people to find their whereabouts since they had won their court case in Montreal, he had obtained information that they had booked tickets and were getting ready to relocate to the Philippines. As he had not since heard anything about an explosion of their property, he was deeply disappointed but remained hopeful that it would soon take place. Getting rid of them for good had always been in the forefront of his mind.

Getting rid of them along with Alfonzo's parents about whom he had almost forgotten, would definitely assure him of the erasure of anyone providing information to the authorities. His first targets were definitely Alfonzo and Martina. As far as for his parents, he felt that they would be so terrified for their lives, witnessing their son and daughter in law's deaths that they would certainly choose to take what they knew of him to their graves.

He intended to eliminate, one by one, anyone who has been involved with Dream Investments, no matter how close or brief their association might have been.

Paolo was well surrounded by a task force that would immediately respond at a snap of his fingers. He would certainly not back off from anything or anyone in carrying on and eliminating his intended targets.

- Cigar? Paolo offered as he lifted and opened a Bolivar cigar box to one to his top lieutenants who was in charge of all of his operations.

They were looking at a big screen in the living room of this summer villa, watching the latest events revealed by the surveillance camera of Alfonzo's home.

- Sure, thank you. Now, what is your plan B Paolo? One of his close advisers asked him. This one hasn't worked as we had expected.

As he took his 24 karat gold lighter from his jacket and offered him light, he looked intently at him, confident about himself that he would certainly not give up but persist until they were done.

- Wait, it is far from being over, trust me.

Chapter 37

Paolo's casualties

Another of Paolo's casualties invaded the media waves; it dragged more attention than Imie Gonzalez's murder. Judge Mercier had been found dead in his luxurious condo situated in the very upscale Plateau area of in Montreal.

His long time partner and fiancée, an attorney had made the gruesome discovery upon her return to town.

She knew of no reason that would have caused him to commit suicide. She suspected that there was a much darker motive hiding behind the gruesome picture that filled the front pages of several local and international newspapers and other media outlets of him found lying dead on his bed. She had no proof for what she was advancing to the media but she certainly believed that her fiancé had been brutally murdered.

It fully absorbed the public's attention as Mercier had been the sitting judge at the time of the non guilty verdict of Alfonzo Pacchiano and Martina Di Salvo. It was the last trial he had presided over as he had stated that he was soon going to retire.

Some medication was found near his bed, mainly pain killers, and a residue of cocaine was discovered on his night stand. A few days later, the coroner established the cause of his death as being a suicide. He had died of a cocaine overdose.

Roberto Lanza, Alfonzo and Martina's lawyer, feared for his life. He suspected that Paolo Di Salvo was surely behind this atrocity and would probably soon come after him. His partners along with all of the personnel of his firm took immediate actions for protection. The place was guarded 24/7 along with their homes and various properties including condos and houses, although most of these were unknown to the majority of citizens. Lanza and his partners owned several condos in the same building in which judge Mercier had lived.

They hired private security guards. They couldn't along with their family members be left on their own anytime or anywhere they would go; probably for the rest of their lives or until Paolo was dead, and the same thing applied to visiting any of their properties.
Paolo Di Salvo was coming after them following the event with the judge and he had no doubt that he himself could soon become himself a target.

As their loyal lawyer and also having developed a very close friendship with the couple, he had attempted for several days following the gruesome discovery of the judge, to make contact with Alfonzo and Martina with the intention of warning them of a more than possible set-up situation that could come up their way and probably would include acts of violence. He strongly feared for their lives as he had not obtained any return to his calls.

The question he kept bouncing around inside his head as to whether or not he should go to the authorities and confess everything he knew of Alfonzo's connections to the mafia boss.

He questioned himself about it for several days despite the fact that it would greatly hurt his reputation as he would unquestionably be served with disbarment which could remove him from the bar association and the practice of law for the rest of his life,
or might it be simpler for him to get on a flight to Hong Kong and ferry his way to their island and personally communicate with them about what was going on?

As he couldn't stand anymore being the effect of these circumstances and increasingly sensing a great fear of danger for his friends, he booked a late flight the same day to Southeast Asia. He didn't give many details as to the exact reason why he was going there but only to say that he wanted to pay his friends a visit and see how they were doing in their new adopted country. No one suspected anything unusual about his sudden decision as he has always maintained good relations with his clients and ex-clients throughout his career.

Roberto Lanza never made it to the intended scheduled flight that night. Despite the fact that since the judge's incident, he had taken all possible security precautions and wore a bullet proof vest all the time, he was shot point blank in the face along with his body guard as they were about to exit the limousine and enter the airport. The limousine driver didn't rush out of the airport. He drove at a steady pace until he reached the highway; nothing suspicious had been clearly spotted by anyone or by the surveillance cameras.

A few days later, three male bodies were discovered by blue collar workers. They were found floating in the St-Lawrence river on the north shore side of the Champlain bridge. They were later identified as being Lanza and his body guard along with the limousine driver. The limousine had been driven into the Great River hundreds of miles away off a privately owned ferryboat. The dumping area was specifically chosen as per the information from radar mapping; it had the deepest gorges in the area. Not sign of it had ever been located.

Chapter 38

The avoidance of a very explosive ambush

A whole series of explosives had been set up. Everything had been set up to respond to what they suspected to be a wireless remote control to be used to trigger the whole lot at the right moment. The personnel assigned for the search, a bomb squad who had been called to survey the area and search in and around the house had soon realised that the agents who had first reached the house were not the intended targets as the explosives had not detonated on their arrival.

After thorough search and nullification of and removal of all the explosive devices and the removal of the surveillance cameras, they gave it an all clear so that Alfonzo and Martina could, if they wished, regain access of their home. They were guaranteed to be protected. Considering that they willingly, in exchange for their guaranteed freedom, had become informants.

It was agreed that any personnel Alfonzo and Martina wished to hire such as maids, cooks and gardeners would be thoroughly screened by the agents. They suspected that Paolo Di Salvo would jump at the occasion to send in unsuspected plants to use in executing his plan when he would judge it appropriate.

As it was already know that Di Salvo was a very vicious and patient man, they wanted to ensure, that once his people were hired Alfonzo and Martina would be able to feel that they could trust them with their lives, then and only then would he send his orders to eliminate them.

Alfonzo's security team looked at all the possibilities and incoming intelligence information, they couldn't afford to make a mistake; the ramifications would be too costly. They finally selected their best nurses, cooks and four more people who they crashed trained as maids and gardeners. However, Alfonzo and Martina would never be told about this personnel selection operation. Only two of them might however cause suspicions and they were the gardeners. One was Japanese and the other American. They looked like two Rambo's on steroids exposing their strength and energy. They "Whey factor" had certainly and furthermore contributed to their muscular body masses.

As soon as they had obtained the green light, they manned up the personnel rapidly. Martina had physical needs of regular treatments and care.

Everything went as planned. The agents were assigned to their domestic duties while keeping close ties with their surveillance operators.

At the time of the hiring, nobody could have thought that they were otherwise than what they were claiming to be. They looked like ordinary people, men and women who did their work and were highly skilled in their areas.

Confident that the contingent of security personnel now in place would do its job, the Interpol agents and their special personnel assigned to the various tasks of clearing the premises of potential dangers withdrew from the area.

Following two weeks of a horrible atmosphere of uncertainty towards their future, Alfonzo and Martina were told that they could finally return home. They would soon be briefed as to the specific roles they would have to play in the projected indictment of Paolo Di Salvo.

The official request for Paolo Di Salvo, along with the top brass of his organization, for extradition had been quietly in the works for quite a while.

Alfonzo and Martina were told to expect, even on a short notice, subpoenas to appear and give their testimony to the court. In the meantime, Alfonzo's parents were soon to join them. They had had suffered throughout an excruciating period of silence since their last phone conversation from Toronto airport while Alfonzo was waiting for his flight to Hong Kong.

While everyone took their duties very seriously and had performed very well since their hiring; the gardeners had been assigned to perform something in addition to their normal duties which was to discretely position sensors and detectors throughout the outside of the property and the rose garden. They soon after assisted in getting a new granite tomb stone where what looked to be simple LED lamps positioned at the two tops ends which would turn on automatically as the sun set to illuminate the engraving.

They were also however color day and night vision cameras that were downright incredible. These latest state of the art cameras could easily see in near darkness full frame of a whole 360 degrees view towards the house and the narrow dock entrance areas. They could at will be oriented to focus towards the tiniest see shell while amplifying its size to make it look like a massive rock.

Every one of these undercover agents had a watch on which they would get immediate alert notification should something be detected. Additionally, they had invisible hearing implants which were wireless receivers from the Interpol office in Manila, Philippines. They knew that it was just a matter of time until Paolo Di Salvo would clearly manifest his intentions. They were ready to tackle the situation.

Chapter 39

Paolo Di Salvo on the look out

After several weeks of hunting, Paolo's experts constantly being on the lookout for a solution which responded to his requirements, their work had finally paid off. They made contact with several hedge fund investment bankers who agreed to involve themselves in the trade operation. They agreed to do the dirty work for him in exchange for irresistible rewards in real estate title deeds. The Real Estate market was still very hot and the money was there waiting to be brought into play.

Following these findings, his brokers, as he called them, had arranged several accounts for him under various pseudonyms which he had hoped would make it difficult for the authorities to track his financial transactions.

The percentage possibilities of being caught were minimal according to his experts and advisers. So, despite the hardship he felt he'd gone through; he was eagerly looking toward that day. He felt a great relief to finally see the tremendous amount of stagnant money sitting in his accounts begin flowing again unsuspectedly throughout several investment portfolios into the financial market.

The range of investments gave him a serious advantage and had left several trackers, employed by his enemy, in the dark. They were certainly frustrated to see that despite their rigorous operation, they lost track of his transactions as quickly as they had detected them originally.

They then turned their research towards investigating the role of several financial institutions which they suspected of corruption and money laundering they felt might be involved in funneling Paolo Di Salvo's money in the marketplace.

They however knew that the banking system was very secretive regarding misconduct and malpractice. Should they attempt to pull some strings and pressure these renowned establishments, they would certainly clam up in response and cite the privacy privilege of their clients. It would certainly be up front as their number one concern and they would be very cautious in divulging anything about their way of banking.

Claiming their client's right to confidentiality had always been in their favour. They always aimed to see their business processes and performance metrics reach the industry best and evaluated as the best practices. Benchmarking was important for them to help them stay at the top of the list.

It would certainly not be the first time where investigators would knock at their doors but they would, using very sophisticated and complex digital systems, purposely but in a very subtle way direct them to a dead-end. It would instantly clear them of any wrong doing while they advocated their innocence.

While the banks operations would appear to be and with the help of calculated marketing ads the best choice within the rest of the remaining options for alternative investments. They had forever reciprocally held a code of silence to protect their important clients.

This was what the Interpol special operation agents had to decipher while continuing to notice detected questionable fiscal dealings with the potential of unearthing and exposing into the light the flaws surrounding their trade procedures which would prove their constant and purposeful divergence from the countries existing fiscal laws.

This was the only way which would finally and positively give them an advantage and allow them to be able to challenge them.
Paolo Di Salvo was a criminal on the loose and they hoped that they could hunt him down and limit his operations until they could accumulate sufficient evidence for him and his accomplices to be taken in for questioning and eventually imprisonment.

Feeling confident that he had once more taken fantastic steps against any potential flare-ups, Paolo Di Salvo returned to his drawing table, sketching different ways as to how he could muzzle his enemies for good. He had not easily swallowed his last defeat. Alfonzo and Martina had damaged the family tradition and he had renounced them as being part of the Di Salvo family.

While none of his victims including Judge Mercier and Imie Gonzalez, had ever violated anything regarding the Cosa Nostra's code of conduct, Paolo considered every one of them, whether directly or indirectly affiliated with the family, as having created a great betrayal towards him.

Alfonzo and Martina had however gotten on his nerves repeatedly and he had found them very costly as he has spent a fortune because of them in order to avoid further problems with the justice system.

Chapter 40

The process of hiring hit men

Paolo Di Salvo would never consider choosing novices while their services were inexpensive in comparison to what he had already spent for his previous successful murder setups.

He would always go with the individuals he has considered as being ultimate professionals. While he already knew and had connections with several hit men he had hired in the past, while holding his opinion of them as being the masters at their jobs, he would however not make use of them for this new assignment.

He knew exactly who to chose. For the judicial authorities, the profiling of these types of top echelon hit men had always been difficult to establish as they had never been caught and therefore were unknown to authorities. This had always been the subject of great concern among the forensic scientists as they were not able to adequately collect, preserve and analyze scientific evidence during the course of an investigation.

Several criminal cases, which many suspected having something to do with Paolo Di Salvo, have turned cold because of their skilled means of vanishing without a trace. It has always been difficult to draw up a complete and conclusive profile on this type of hit man. Paolo found his men. Accessing the private island had once proved to be possible but this time it would not be that easy. But as he had figured it out along with his experts, while the possibilities of success would not be one hundred percent guaranteed, it was worth it to take a shot.

For this operation, nothing would be neglected, the money was not an issue for him; Alfonzo Pacchiano and Martina Di Salvo were. His team would soon depart aboard a rented yacht and navigate towards Ariara Island.

Using the latest state of the art technological apparatus currently on the market consisting of night goggles, hearing aids and waterproof guns, they would make their way to the island a few hours after sun set.

Upon their arrival close to the island's shore, they would first wait to get the information from an inaudible drone that would survey the area. It would send information in order to immediately warn of potential threats and let them know when the time would be right.

Chapter 41

The taciturn enemy

A few hours after sun set, as everything was clear for them to engage, they got off the boat and eased themselves into the water. In pitch darkness, all dressed in scuba clothing, they slowly moved one stroke at the time. Doing their best to avoid even the smallest of noises, they slowly swam their way to the dock entrance. They hid under the dock and waited for their instructions. As they got the all clear signal from Paolo's ship that was anchored on the south eastern shore of the island, they loaded their guns and crept towards the house.

Everyone in the household had gone to bed except for Martina who was sitting on the front veranda reading the latest international news on her tablet.

Amongst the usual sound of the wave's rhythmic rolling onto the shore, she heard some twigs snapping which dragged her attention away from her reading. She quietly deposited her tablet on the side table and pulled her gun from under her plaid blanket.

All the undercover agents were already on the lookout prior for unusual sounds such as the one Martina had just heard. They had already been warned that there was a definite intrusion as they had received clear signals that a drone had been detected hovering over the area. They discretely moved outside and toward the back veranda of the house.

They gradually dispersed around the house until the two gardeners stood one at each end of the front veranda. With their night vision goggles, they had clearly detected active infrared lights moving towards the house. As these got closer, they could distinguish that they were two tall individuals and according to the latest imagery obtained from the tomb stone cameras, they were heavily armed. Martina had become an easy target. The hit men were all eyes on her. Before she realised it, as it was still dark all around, two men had aimed their riffles towards her.

One of them suddenly twisted around and fell to the ground while the other hurriedly retraced his steps back to the dock. One of the maids pulled Martina's wheelchair inside while the American gardener walked towards the man he had just shot. The rest of the team continued to survey the area on the lookout for additional intruders.

He dragged the motionless body up onto the front veranda where he pulled out his LED flashlight to see if he was showing any vital signs. A long trail of blood marked the stairs steps and spread throughout the area where he had laid the wounded man. As he yanked off his mask, the man stared back at him in excruciating pain. He had gotten hit in his neck and was bleeding profusely.

In an attempt to get information from him, the gardener lifted him by the shoulders to force him to speak up while the nurse examined the state of his wound. She silently nodded her head indicating that he did not have a chance of surviving. The man's only response to the questioning was a whisper in his last breath with a strong Russian accent Paolo Di Salvo's name. His eyes rolled over inside his head. He was dead.

The nurse then dispatched a request to the agency for the removal of the body. They would perform DNA tests and take his fingerprints in order to properly identify the man.

One of the agents arrived on the scene and dropped the now deactivated drone beside the dead man.

- We have located the stool pigeon. It shouldn't be too long before "pick up", said one of the cooks.

- Great, when this is all over, we will celebrate it with your best meal.

They exchanged a smile and turned their attention toward chasing the other hit man who, per the infrared lights was no longer being detected within the immediate vicinity of the house.

While they would continue to carry out their search, the two maids would stay behind.

They walked throughout the property arriving at the dock where the hit man was holding his breath under the dock. He was close to being discovered.

This is when the Japanese suggested that two of them stay in the dock area in case they might be able to spot him.

He heard everything and he knew that he had no chance if he even dared to make a move. He sent a codified request to the yacht to abort the mission and got no response.

Everyone else had been woken up by Martina who obviously was in a complete state of shock. They had suddenly come to the shocking realisation that they had all along been surrounded by a team of highly trained security agents who had just prevented Martina's murder.

Later that night, The Philippine National Police – Maritime Group – vessels surrounded Paolo Di Salvo's yacht. They ordered the Captain to stop the engines and for him and his crew to come out on deck with their hands up. They warned that they were the police and that the yacht was going to be boarded. Any resistance would be met with deadly force.

The police attempted to board but a profusion of gun shots in their direction showed that they were badly outnumbered. Paolo would certainly not surrender easily.

Instead of following their instructions, some of the crew and Paolo's body guards had fired on the police.

A running battle ensued which lasted for more than one hour, this continued until one of Paolo's guards took the situation into his own hands. He repeatedly threw grenades towards the National Police ships. The damage sustained was beyond anything these ships could tolerate from this ravaging attack. Anyone looking on from a distance would see a very spectacular view of burning ships on fire and flames rising to great heights and lighting up the night sky. Paolo's yacht rapidly fled the scene as other National Police ships came to the rescue of their comrades. The flames could be seen miles away.

The policemen who were lucky to have survived the assault were rescued from the blazing ships but unfortunately many had not been so lucky.

Additional ships were soon to take up the chase.

Chapter 42

Chasing the last hit man

As the sun rose, nothing revealing the presence or the whereabouts of the second hit man had been found.

The two agents standing at the nearby dock patiently waited to see if anything out of the ordinary would happen.

The sun was scorching and the hit man had been standing in the water for more than 24 hrs now and as he was still in his scuba suit, he had begun to feel the increasing unbearable heat. He was becoming dehydrated and extremely thirsty. He knew that he had no chance of surviving the situation if he did not get out of there soon. Due to the regular rhythmic sounds of the waves which were being strongly pushed by increasingly blustery weather, he calculated that he should wait until the rain came on shore to escape.

Thunder clouds were rapidly gathering over his head and he knew that it would be his last chance if he wanted to survive.

A huge wave came in his direction and he plunged into it in the hope of being pulled further out to the sea. He didn't know how much oxygen remained in his tank but took the precaution of holding his breath as long as he could to save it as much as possible until he would see the shores of a neighbouring island. While the power of the waves was unforgiving, he succeeded in escaping from the island.

He hoped to be able to make some contact with an ally who would come to his rescue.

Four of the undercover agents extended the area of their search by boat over a larger neighbouring area which comprised of the nearby uninhabited small islands suspecting that he might have been able to reach one of their shores.

The police ships were getting closer but then as they saw a helicopter appearing on the horizon coming their way, they had to take cover as people inside it were armed with rifles and were aiming and shooting at them.

While some of his guards were shooting at the police from the ship and the helicopter, Paolo and his men were waiting to evacuate the ship. The helicopter descended onto the heli pad situated in the front of the vessel and everyone got onboard.

As they watched the helicopter swiftly flying away, the ship exploded into two separate pieces and sank rapidly under the waters. The four agents heard the explosion as they carried on with their search for the hit man despite the sea's raging waves pounding their boat. As they approached the nearest island, they finally spotted someone dressed in scuba gear showing no signs of life, lying on its beach.

They got off their boat and swam to the shore. As they approached him, he gave no sign of life until he heard the sound of their guns being activated.

The hit man couldn't do anything but surrender. He was dehydrated, exhausted and completely defenceless. They took his weapons away from him, handcuffed him and brought him to the boat.

Later the same day, the hit man was brought to Interpol HQ in Hong Kong where an intensive interrogation would soon ensue. Under heavy surveillance by armed guards, he received intravenous fluids and was fed.

He was of Russian origin as was his partner. As he fit all the requirements needed for them to be able to interrogate him, two Interpol agents started the questioning.

What they found about him was appalling. This man was now operating under an identity other than his own. After checking in their data base, not finding anything related to him from his finger prints, they suspected mutilation of his ten fingertips. It was not something new within the forensic world; they had been cautioned over several years, that suspects may try to dodge their past by altering their fingertip identities.

After several hours of nonstop excruciating questioning, he finally confessed that he had the ends cut off of all ten of his fingertips; the skin then pulled back together over them and stitched.

He had returned to work for his mafia boss after managing to escape jail years ago for involvement in one of Paolo's criminal schemes. He was too important for them to let him rot in jail. Paolo succeeded in bribing the jail director to let him go free. It had not however been a straight money payoff. Blackmail and threats were also used as part of the deal, making him understand that his family members could easily disappear if he did not cooperate.

At first, he would not budge; he received repeated warnings that it would only be a matter of lifting a finger for a sniper to eliminate every member of his family. Under this pressure, the jail director finally gave up and made the arrangements for the prisoner to escape disguised as a newly hired prison guard. He just walked out the front door of the prison. Vladislav Stepanov became a free man. He soon reconnected with Paolo and continued with his criminal activities. Stepanov had been provided with a new set of identification and even undergone several surgeries involving a nose job and face lift. He also had a very visible scar removed from his chin which was the reminder of a brutal knife fight with a rival gang member.

As he finally made known his true identity, he was in his mid-fifties, a man who had lived within the criminal circle for years. It exposed a man who had a very hefty and violent life history.

He was certainly part of the new breed of hit man. He had committed several murders, attempted murders, involved in drug trafficking, human smuggling for the purpose of prostitution and various types of casino money laundering activities. However, he had only gotten caught and jailed for attempted murder. For all of the other crimes he had ever committed, he had never been caught.

After letting him know how crucial it had become for the authorities to nail Paolo Di Salvo, he was given the choice of guaranteed immunity if he would testify against Paolo or imprisonment for life. He preferred the freedom incentive offered in exchange for volunteering and turning over everything he knew about Paolo Di Salvo, all of his associates, his activities and connections.

The agents interrogating him were finally able to join the dots regarding years of several unsolved crimes up to this day. They now were finally capable of constructing a comprehensive org board of all Di Salvo's businesses and accomplices.

Chapter 43

Fleeing the scene

All aboard one of Di Salvo's private jets which later landed in Aeroporto Vincenzo Florio were then driven to Marsala; they regrouped at Paolo's summer villa. He and his accomplices had no clue as to what had happened to his hit men and from the reports of the police activity; he doubted that they had completed the job he assigned them. But he couldn't confirm anything as he had lost contact with them soon after they confirmed they were closing in on the shore of Alfonzo's island.

At the same time, he strongly hoped that they had pulled it off. He wanted a rest from hunting the Pacchiano family.

Soon the media reported on this mysterious event which had occurred off the coast of the island with the Italian police reporting that it concerned the most wanted man in the country. A whooping cash award was offered to anyone coming forward to provide information that would indicate Paolo Di Salvo whereabouts or anyone who might have recently witnessed anything related to his activities; they also welcomed anyone who would prefer to anonymously provide the information.

Paolo knew that his days were numbered if he didn't quickly act. He knew that he had to disappear for a while as the police along with several agencies would soon track him down. He had his wife and kids flown to the Bahamas where they would be safe until he could figure out a solution to safely join them at a later date.

For the Interpol agents, it was vital that they gather adequate and sufficient information to nail and incarcerate Paolo. The Italian government's justice department had been warned and advised of Paolo's criminal activities. For years, they had strongly encouraged greater surveillance and infiltration amongst his empire as he was suspected of being the no 1 cause behind several numerous unsolved casualties within the financial world.

Despite their assurance that they had taken action, in order to gather intelligence about him, it had never materialized. Di Salvo was someone who in Italy was considered to be the supreme god way above the pope and for good reasons; he was more involved in their lives.

He had donated huge amounts of money to several non profit organizations, foundations and charities that would have never been able to survive without his generosity.

While it was certainly known by the general population that he was the top Sicilian mafia boss, they reluctantly refused to agree that he was the devil that many news reporters attempted to label him.

For some of them, their lives had been shortened by a very outraged and offended Paolo. There had been merciless and deadly consequences for any one of them who had attempted, despite their imminent danger, to clearly expose the real purpose shadowing behind his hand-outs and conning everyone in return. Paolo's reputation was as sacred as any of the religious based principles his family has followed for generations. No one could mess with him without harsh consequences.

Other reporters had given up, witnessing first hand some of their colleagues unexpectedly disappearing for no reason or found lifeless near their homes or in their cars. They no longer wanted to have any part of the conversation. While they knew what they could state was true, they feared for their lives as they had over time suffered psychological duress and intimidation.

Since the information regarding his hit men kept streaming within the intelligence community, the missing puzzle pieces had soon been put together. Paolo's underground activities were undeniably extremely sophisticated. Without this significant information, it would have been a situation of looking for a four leaf clover in grassland.

The two nurses and the maids, Interpol agents, stayed behind at Alfonzo's home to oversee everyone's security until they would receive the positive news of Paolo Di Salvo's incarceration. The two gardeners soon rejoin them. Everyone was at the ready and on the lookout for any suspicious presence coming on shore.

Paolo Di Salvo's wife and kids were detained for questioning soon after they had landed in the Bahamas. She clearly manifested fear for own her and her kid's lives as she knew that her husband would take immediate action to eliminate them if he found that she had provided information.

Paolo soon received a text message that his wife and kids were in trouble and he strongly suspected that they would be restricted communicating except under surveillance tap with him or anyone of his connections.

Chapter 44

The trailing of the fugitives

Paolo Di Salvo was not looking forward to the long flight over the Atlantic Ocean; however he was looking forward to his safe landing in Havana.

Intelligence traced Paolo Di Salvo on his way to Cuba which indicated to them that he would certainly seek asylum in that country. They figured out that he wished to get closer to his family and this was the best option he had to narrow the physical distance between him and his family. While he had not been in contact with his wife for days, two of his highly skilled operatives had been dispatched to the Bahamas. He was looking to jump on the best opportunity that would be presented to him to quickly get them on a plane and reunite with them. This would however leave traces of casualties.

As he later on found out that his wife and kids were confined in their rented condo and under surveillance 24/7, he felt that he didn't have the choice of addressing the matter this way.

Several Interpol agents of Cuban descent, identifying themselves as Canadian tourists, flew from Miami and had landed at the airport. They were not spotted by Di Salvo's people. Looking like ordinary men and women tourists and two as baggage handlers, they were assigned to wait inside and outside the airport until further instructions

Having succeeded in hacking the outside and inside surveillance cameras, it was just a matter of time to finally catch their fugitive. As soon as he landed on an isolated tarmac, a bulletproof SUV rushed to the plane and hurried to get away as fast as possible from the airport.

The baggage handlers got in their cars and the chase began.

The SUV purposely made its way towards the city's narrow busy streets with lots of tourists filling in the restaurants, bars and shops in the areas. The SUV finally stopped near a bar where Paolo Di Salvo was seen getting out of it surrounded by heavily armed men and transferring into a local vintage car.

The agents could see that the SUV followed him for security reasons. They had to keep track of him and were doing their best to locate his destination.

There was no rational explanation they could come up with as to why he got into this car until they realised the meaning of the second letter on the licence plate. "A" being on a white licence plate indicated that it was related to a government minister, provincial official and or other important state person.

As some of the tourists were in the area where Alfonzo got on the other car, they'd been able to take some photographic shots of the inside of the car. They soon identified the individual person sitting at the back of the vintage car waiting for him. The passenger was Angela Krämer, the retired Swiss banker's widow. She had been a direct accomplice in Paolo's effort towards the indictment of Alfonzo Pacchiano and Martina Di Salvo during their trial.

Since he'd made contact with her following her husband's suicide on Alfonzo's yacht, she rapidly realised, from the man's generously compensating for her husband's loss, that they were sharing more common enrichment conceptual strategies than she had ever thought. She had greatly enriched herself by her association with Paolo Di Salvo in Dutch land deals in the underground financial market.

Paolo was on his way to meet the officials to bust his way in. He hoped that it would finally give him the peace of mind he wished-for since he had fled his country. Nobody would be able to drag him out from the country. He would then be able to resume his business from there, get his wife and kids to the island and return to normal operation.

Chapter 45

The final winning strategy

The Di Salvo family became reunited. His team rescued his wife and kids during very stormy weather. It was pouring cats and dogs and the power went out which disabled all the security systems and surveillance cameras around the condo. While there had been calls for reinforcements as they suspected Paolo would try to pull this off, his response had been swift. All the security guards had been eliminated. His team jumped on the occasion of the storm and yanked them out within minutes after killing the body guards and were soon on their way to Cuba.

Everything had been quiet for several months. However, Interpol had been silently brewing a strategy in order to incarcerate the Mafia boss. The European Court of Justice finally responded and they went after him to seize his entire assets. Paolo's lawyers weren't able to make any dent in this case. Paolo started to feel an increased sentiment of distrust towards them.

As the European Court of Justice put more heat on their case, he felt that if he didn't go to the Court and personally address this matter himself, that he would be completely screwed. The Italian government, under a severe reality adjustment where they would be publicly denounced as being direct benefactor of the Mafia boss, had been strongly encouraged enough to feed him false reports on what was going on, so he couldn't trust his lawyers anymore.

Paolo felt he needed to go over there and find out what was going on for himself. No one was supposed to know that he was going to Luxembourg to plead his innocence but somebody leaked the information to the European Court so they knew exactly when he was going to arrive.

As they were approaching the airport, the pilot of the private plane was given coordinates by airport officials to make sure that he landed on a runway away from the major area of the terminal. This was to ensure that when they closed in to make their arrest, there would not be any danger for anybody else in the area.

The set up worked. Everything around was quiet, only a few luggage handlers driving towards the terminal made their way close to the plane. One of them parked close to the plane waiting to download their baggage. As he gave the signal that he was ready to open the luggage doors, a squad of officers ran out of the main airport area from different exits and immediately surrounded the plane. No one in the plane could have suspected that such operation could ever take place without their knowledge.

Paolo Di Salvo had finally been caught and arrested.

Chapter 46

The European Court of Justice

The six undercover agents who stayed with the Pacchiano family were given the information that they were now relieved of their duties.

As they announced to the family that they would soon leave, the two gardeners pulled off their facial masks to reveal that they were in fact the two investigators that Lanza, Alfonzo's lawyer had hired for Martina's rescue.

- We couldn't let him go without justice, they said.

***

Alfonzo and Martina were amongst many witnesses who had been subpoenaed to go to Luxembourg and make their depositions in front of the European Court of Justice.

All the while, Alfonzo's parents intensively watched both of them at the witness bench, living again every part of that incident that brought them to that point which, to say the least, had been a very rough ride.

The prospect of finally witnessing Paolo Di Salvo being served with a guilty verdict was what they had been hoping to see for a long time. They had wished they could have witnessed the same sentence to the man's uncle who had controlled them soon after Alfonzo was born.

A few months later, he was handed a sentence of life in prison with no chance of parole. All his connections had received the same sentence.

A few days later Paolo Di Salvo was found dead in his cell. The cause of his sudden death has never been released.

There was a rumor that one of his own hit men had killed him because it was thought he had given data to the authorities that led to him being arrested. No one was ever convicted of his murder.

From the author:

Thank you for reading my book. I hope that you've enjoyed the experience.

You are welcome to write your review and rating on the site from which you purchased this book.

They are always welcome.

Thank you,
Claire

P.S.: There are many other stories available to you on my author page, each one of them written to entertain you. Enjoy!